Turbulent Seas

Violet Heart
Laura Kitchell
Sara Murphy
Mae Powers

Published by
Melange Books, LLC
White Bear Lake, MN 55110
www.melange-books.com

Ayprial's Desire, Copyright © 2008-2011 Violet Heart
Forever, Copyright © 2009-2011 Laura Kitchell
Sea Angel, Copyright © 2009-2011 Laura Kitchell
A Prince's Tail , Copyright © 2009-2011 Sara Murphy
Turbulent Hearts, © 2009-2011 Mae Powers

ISBN 978-1-61235-156-8

Names, characters, and incidents depicted in this book are products of the author's imagination or are used fictitiously. Any resemblance to actual events, locales, organizations, or persons, living or dead, is entirely coincidental and beyond the intent of the author or the publisher. No part of this book may be reproduced or transmitted in any form or by any means, electronic or mechanical, including photocopying, recording, or by any information storage and retrieval system, without permission in writing from the publisher.

Editor: Nancy Schumacher
Copy Editor: Taylor Evans
Format Editor: Mae Powers
Cover Artist: A. Bratt

Turbulent Seas Digest

Ayprial's Desire, Violet Heart
Dr. Peter Bastian didn't know what he was in for when he pulled a mermaid from a commercial fishing net. Neither did she.

Forever, By Laura Kitchell
Caught in the rocks during a terrible storm, a mermaid gets rescued by an unlikely human – a novelist turned lighthouse keeper. Through the course of the night, he helps her heal and offers friendship; but what will come when the storm passes and the light of day offers her a chance to return to the sea? And can he let her go?

Sea Angel, Laura Kitchell
A mermaid faces a painful death if she cannot find her calling and mate within the hour. The only male in the area is a sea-angel, the one creature who can rob her of gills and tail with a single touch. Will she die alone, having never known passion's bliss? Or can she risk his touch and take the chance of drowning in his arms?

A Prince's Tail , Sara Murphy
After being cheated on by her fiancée, Maggie returns to her cottage by the sea to batten down the hatches and mend her broken heart. Hearing the call from his mate, Tarman braves the wrath of his royal parents and the fury of a hurricane to find her. When Maggie finds the injured Tarman in her boat house she tends his wounds and he heals her heart.

Turbulent Hearts, Mae Powers
When Taroc rescues a beautiful alien woman from a watery death, the turbulent seas of his mind, heart, and body are enflamed by her completely. But will she reciprocate his feelings, or return to the sea of stars she fell from?

Ayprial's Desire
by
Violet Heart

Dr. Peter Bastian didn't know what he was in for when he pulled a mermaid from a commercial fishing net. Neither did she.

www.geocities.com/violethearterotica/main.html

- violetheart@exis.net

Ayprial's Desire
By
Violet Heart

Chapter One

Ayprial's tail twitched with irritation. Planting a hand on the fin to still it, she asked her mentor, "Why don't you know? You're my teacher. If you can't tell me, how am I supposed to learn?"

Rysha sliced an angry arm through the water. "It doesn't matter! To survive, we don't need to know about outside things." She flipped her long white braid over a shoulder and looked away.

Ayprial crossed her arms, trying not to glare at her stubborn teacher. "Aren't we past mere survival? I mean, look around." She swung her arm in a wide arc, taking in the elaborate city with its glowing coral and harvested neon fish casting light everywhere. "Our society is sophisticated. Intelligent. We have a complex communications network with the other cities along the drop-off zone. There's no reason we should be closed-minded. So why aren't we making an effort to better understand our world?"

"I don't have time for this," said Rysha, packing shells into her sack. Her seafoam gray eyes reflected metallic flecks in the light streaming down from a glow worm lantern.

"Then you won't mind if I do some exploring on my own."

Her mentor turned on her, hands fisted on hips where the skin of her torso met her tail. "I most certainly do. It's not safe outside the city walls. You've been sheltered and don't know what's out there."

Frustration made Ayprial's gills flutter, sending tiny pearlescent bubbles into her hair. She pushed the billowing mass of black tendrils behind her. "It's not my fault I don't have a family to lead me into the outlands. I've been asking *you* to show me for years."

Rysha trembled. At first, Ayprial thought her teacher shook with anger, but a flash of fear transformed the older mermaid's features a moment before she lowered the veil of indifference back into place. "Of course, it's not your fault you lost your parents at such a young age. But I'm not the one to take you out of the city."

"Well, I'm an adult now—"

"And time for you to put aside your childish interest in creatures and plants that will play no part in your life as wife and mother. You should concentrate on finding your lifemate."

Oh! Ayprial wanted to scream. Her teacher toted the sack and began to swim toward the orphanage, and she followed. "It's not childish. And it's not just about creatures and plants. I want to know about currents and tides, why it's so bright near the surface and what makes the coral glow. Why some days it glows brighter than others— Oof!" Her pet triggerfish, Pentri, rammed her in the stomach, halting her.

Rysha didn't turn. She merely shook her head and lifted a dismissing hand as she continued on her way.

She doesn't care, thought Ayprial, stroking Pentri's snout to calm him. Tomorrow, she would turn twenty-two and reach her majority. The orphanage would no longer offer her a place to stay. And Rysha would say goodbye.

No doubt with great relief.

Ayprial had no intension of sticking around for them to kick her out. She'd go to another city. One where nobody knew her. Where she could begin anew, as a person of worth. She couldn't be the only merperson who wanted to learn about their world. Perhaps she would meet someone who would teach her. Explore with her. Share her curiosity.

Yes. She had no reason to stay.

"I'm leaving," she told her pet. "Where should I go? Krypta or Stryka?"

Pentri studied her a moment then turned to face the orphanage.

"No. I don't care that the day is coming to an end. I'm not staying." She picked up a shell. "Ridges side—Krypta. Smooth side—Stryka."

The fish spun around to watch.

Ayprial flipped the shell, which toppled end over end to land silently on the silt of the ocean floor. Smooth side up.

"Stryka it is." Joyful anticipation mingled with fear of the unknown. Rysha had seemed terrified at the idea of leaving the boundaries of their home city of Entra. Ayprial couldn't ignore that. But she couldn't stay, either. To give in to fear meant living the rest of her life with regrets.

She looked one last time toward the orphanage. She had arrived there with nothing; she would leave with nothing. No friends. No possessions. Not even fond memories.

Turning her back on the place, she nodded to Pentri. "I'll understand if you want to stay."

Her pet darted, bouncing off her chest then snuggling under her arm.

She chuckled. "Let's go."

With her heart sad from a disappointing past, but her eyes on a bright and hopeful future, Ayprial swam for the enormous arching columns that formed the city's gateway.

* * * *

"Look, I have to go today. All the sensors are in place, and we need those readings for Monday's report. If you're sick, you're sick. But I still have to go." Peter Bastian shook his head at the sight of the sun peeking over the horizon. It sucked! He really needed an assistant today of all days. Scuffing the sole of his sneaker along a board of the dock, he cut his gaze to the steel-hulled, sixty-foot retired navy-vessel-turned-research boat that the captain was readying for departure.

"I'm sorry, man," said Ben. He sneezed so loudly, Peter jerked and thrust his cell phone at arm's length. When Ben spoke again, it came across as a mumble.

Peter put the phone to his ear. "What?"

"I said, transmit the numbers to the database as you pull the readings, and I'll access them here at home to plug into the report. Susie can print it tomorrow at the office. That way, we can both take tomorrow off."

A three-day weekend. Now, that sounded good. "I'd rather have you here on the boat, but I guess I can settle for you finishing the report."

"Believe me, you don't want me there." Ben blew his nose.

Peter sighed just as the captain fired up the boat's engine. "All right. Take it easy, and I'll see you Monday." He pressed the end button and dropped the phone in his shorts pocket.

"You need help with that, Dr. Bastian?" The captain eyed Peter's bag while climbing down from the bridge.

"No, thanks, Jack. I got it." He stepped onto the dive platform to sling the green canvas bag off his shoulder and set it just inside the transom. It landed with a thud.

"Geez, Doc. What ya got in there, anyway?" The captain hopped past the last three steps, his feet hitting the deck with a smack.

"Some personal stuff. Last week, Captain Shaw ran us through a squall. Ben and I had to help on deck, and I got soaked. So, from now on, I'm bringing a change of clothes and stuff for a shower. Just in case." Peter shivered with the memory.

Jack shrugged then continued below decks.

Asshole. Peter couldn't stand Jack Serfass, but he didn't have much say about who captained the boat. At least he wouldn't have to interact with him on this trip. The tech team had set sensor recorders the day before and entered the GPS coordinates for the captain. While the captain ran the boat from the bridge, Peter could sit in the lab with the door closed and operate the electronic equipment so integral to his work.

Since he would need to transmit data back to shore, he fetched a power booster from a transport van. He boarded the boat and let Captain Serfass know they could leave when the engine warmed. Tossing his bag in a stateroom, he carried the power booster down the hall, went into the lab and kicked the door closed.

Alone in his element, he took a deep cleansing breath and looked around with a smile. He moved around the lab with thoughtful care, flicking switches and pressing buttons to start the machines. Soon the room whined and hummed. He loved that sound. While booting the computer, thumps sounded topside. Jack had pulled the ropes free from their mooring.

Peter looked out the window and stared at the white and gray buildings of the Virginia Oceanographic Research Foundation. Home sweet home, he thought. The engine revved, vibrating the entire vessel. Out the window,

Norfolk slipped past, left behind as he headed out to the deep ocean. Norfolk Canyon held the answers. He just knew it.

As the computer screen flashed to life, he reviewed the numbers from their last three runs. This fourth set would give them the whole picture. His report would make history.

He didn't expect fame or riches. Just a deeper understanding of the mysterious ocean. Water covered two-thirds of earth, yet they knew so little of life there. He and his colleagues had suspected the intelligence of dolphins and whales for years, but now he stood on the edge of cracking their language. It was all in the numbers. His heart thrummed with excitement. He really wanted Ben with him today. They had worked so hard for this.

He turned on the speakers and listened to whale song. The pitch. The resonation. The pattern. When broken down by the computer, the language became distinct. All he had to come up with was the key to unlock the meaning.

He listened, running calculations through the equipment all the way out to the canyon. Jack knocked on the door when they arrived at the first sensor. On his way out, Peter grabbed a retracted collector. He bounded up the steps and across the deck to the stern of the boat.

The captain maneuvered the vessel, and Peter pulled the steel collector to its full length. When the bloated white float attached to the sensor came in range, he dipped the end of the pole into the water and hooked the recorder.

As it left the water, a gray nose followed.

Peter blinked, almost dropping the sensor. He lifted the float higher, and the nose rose. A dolphin lifted from the waves and clicked at him. It looked right at him! Three high clicks followed by two lower rolling trills and a guttural huff.

Peter scowled. Was the animal talking to him? He pulled the recorder out of the water and set it on the deck, laying the collector against the transom. Leaning over, he stared down at the dolphin, which repeated its noises.

Three high clicks. Peter scowled deeper and thought back to his internship at Sea World in Florida. Didn't that mean *come*? Was the dolphin asking him to come with it? He shook his head. That was crazy.

Jack put the boat in gear and motored half a mile to the next sensor. The dolphin swam alongside. When Peter lowered the collector, a second dolphin joined the first. It followed the sensor out of the water, like the first had, and repeated the noises. The exact same noises! *Shit! What's going on?*

He set the sensor next to the other and put down the pole. Leaning over the transom, he imitated the three high clicks and tilted his head. The two dolphins went wild, leaping and spinning. Before he could explore further, the captain moved on toward the third sensor.

The two animals followed. Peter watched, fascinated, as they chattered excitedly to one another. Even though he couldn't hear their sounds since they swam under the surface, he could tell that they obviously held a conversation. He'd never seen anything like it.

He ran to the lab and snatched his camcorder out of a case. As he ran back, he prayed they hadn't gone. Far from it. Before he could reach the stern, one leapt high out of the water. For a second, he thought it would land on the deck, and he came to a sliding halt. It caught sight of him and arced to the water with a loud CHIT-CHIT-CHIT-CHIT!

"Huh!" Peter fumbled to turn on the camcorder. Walking to the transom, he checked to make sure it held a fresh tape. It did. His heart began to beat hard as he leaned out and began recording.

One of the dolphins leapt out of the boat's wake and let out a single, long squeal. He knew that sound, too. *Yes*. The animal said *yes*. Yes to what? Yes to record them? Or yes, he headed where they wanted him to go?

At the third sensor, a third dolphin followed the device up out of the water and repeated the 'come' message. And something pale and small swam just behind it. What the heck was that? Then it leapt out of the water. A triggerfish! He'd never seen a triggerfish jump like that! Did it check him out? *What in the world?*

The triggerfish leapt again then went like a shot to a strange swirl in the water and jumped again. Peter followed a line past the fish and saw nothing. Damn it! Why were these creatures acting so weird?

Jack yelled from the bridge. "There's a heck of a wreck down there. Looks like something big is caught on it. I thought it was a big school of fish, but it just waves back and forth. I can't really tell what's hooked to that wreck."

Was that what the animals tried to tell him? But what was up with the triggerfish?

He didn't have time to ponder longer, though, because Jack continued on toward the last sensor. The dolphins didn't follow this time.

Chapter Two

Peter turned off the camcorder and wondered at the strange behavior. It plagued him, even as he shrugged and retrieved the final sensor. "Hey, Jack! Come help me carry these to the lab!" he hollered over the roar of the engine.

"Just a sec!" yelled the captain. He set the boat to idle, and the motor quieted to a gentle humming rumble.

Peter retracted the collector pole and tucked it under his arm then picked up the sensors marked *number one* and *number two*. Before heading to the lab, he scanned the gentle waves glinting under the high, mid-afternoon sun. Nothing. No movement whatsoever.

In the lab, he directed Jack to set the last two sensors on a table. "Do me a favor."

"What's that?" asked the captain.

"Instead of heading back right away, why don't you set anchor and have lunch?" Peter's stomach knotted.

"Why?" Jack went to the door, but didn't leave.

"Call it a hunch. I want to listen to these before we head back."

"Okay." The captain turned as if to leave, but looked over his shoulder and said, "That was quite a show those fish gave. Huh?"

Fish? "They're not fish. They're mammals, like us. And yes, it was."

"Man, what I wouldn't give for a fishing pole and a fighting chair."

Peter wanted to send his fist into the man's face. "I've got work."

"Yeah, okay. Let me know what you want to do after you finish whatever it is you do with those things." Jack left, closing the door behind him.

"Idiot." Peter set sensors one and two on the table and lifted the guard to keep the expensive equipment from rolling off the table, in case the boat pitched unexpectedly. He mumbled, "Catch all the sport fish you want, but leave the mammals alone."

He studied the four recorders. Normally, he would enter the data in order, but something urged him to listen to *number three* first. He removed it from the float, dried the outer water case, then cracked open the device and retrieved the sound chip. Plugging it into the computer's adaptor, he tapped his foot with impatience.

He started up the program he and Ben had designed for this project, and began downloading. Crossing his arms over his chest, he paced from one end of the lab to the other and back until the program beeped its completion. Like a kid on Christmas, he raced for the keyboard. Not taking the time to sit, he bent over the desk and typed in a string of commands then tapped it into the speakers.

The computer automatically filtered out dead spaces in the recording. The screen told him sensor number three contained two hour's worth of sounds matching criteria set in the program parameters, then fed the information through the speakers.

The first ten minutes held standard whale song. Then something strange happened. He thought he heard words. Human language. It sounded panicked. Female. It couldn't be right.

Tapping on the keyboard, he learned the sounds began a little after nine o'clock. Too late at night for divers. The female voice continued for thirty minutes, growing weaker and weaker. Finally, only occasional sounds occurred while the screen showed the time intervals—ten thirty, eleven forty-five, two o'clock a.m. The last sound came at eleven o'clock.

Only an hour ago!

His heart pounding, he raced through the boat like his life depended on it. He found Jack finishing lunch in the galley. "We have to go back!"

"You're ready to head back? That didn't take long." The captain stood.

"No! Not back to shore. Back to the coordinates of the third sensor. You still have them in the GPS, right?" He had to calm down.

"Sure. You want to go right now?"

His stomach flipped. "Yes. Immediately." He had to find out what made those sounds. He suspected it was caught in whatever was waving in the current above that wreck.

"No problem. It's overtime, and I'm fine with that." Jack grinned and left.

Peter's mind raced. Quickly, he slapped a piece of American cheese between two slices of bread and crammed half in his mouth on his way back to the lab. In a flurry of activity, he gathered his dive gear from a locker, ate the last of his sandwich and went up on deck. He dropped the gear next to strapped tanks under the bridge then tripped down the stairs to get to his stateroom.

Okay, he *really* had to calm down.

Changing into a swimsuit, he left his clothes in a heap on the floor. He arrived back on deck as the boat began to slow. A dolphin sprang into the air and nodded its head at him. He waved.

With the precision that came from years of diving, he squeezed into his wetsuit, zipped on his boots, and strapped his dive knife to the inside of his leg in no time. When they arrived over the wreck, he had his buoyancy compensator strapped to a tank and his regulator sealed to the tank's K valve.

Pulling a rebar wreck anchor out of a deck compartment, he yelled toward the bridge. "Let me know when to drop it."

Captain Serfass gave a wave, put the engine in gear and maneuvered the boat. "Now!"

Peter tossed the anchor over the port side and stepped back, letting the rope play out from the compartment. After a few minutes, the anchor hit bottom. He took the slack, wrapped two loops around a winch drum and waited. The rope jerked and jolted before the boat came to a halt.

"We're hooked on the wreck. Give the rope a hard yank!" called Jack.

Peter freed them. They needed to get this on the first try, or they would run out of time. He could feel it!

"Looks like the anchor snagged whatever that thing is," said the captain. "The sonar display shows the shadow's pulled tight. Go ahead and turn on the winch."

He flipped the switch, and the drum creaked and groaned as it spun the rope. The captain came to stand at his side, and they watched in silence to see what the anchor dragged to the surface. The edge of a net poked out of the waves and headed for the boat.

"Shit!" Jack sprinted for the bridge. "If that thing gets caught in the prop, we're screwed!"

Peter switched off the winch, and Captain Serfass shut down the engine. The net sank as the anchor weighted it under the boat.

"Come give me a hand," Peter called, his heart pounding now. Something waited in that net. Something special.

Jack scampered down from the bridge and hauled the oxygen tank to the transom. Heaving it over, he set the equipment onto the dive platform.

Peter hopped over and eased his mask over his head. One of the dolphins came forward and rested its nose on the ledge. He chuckled. "Can you grab my weight belt and fins?"

"Sure," said the captain. "That fish seems awfully tame. What do you think is down there?"

"I don't know." He fit the snorkel mouthpiece over his teeth and sank his face in the water, searching for anything that might pose an immediate threat. The other two dolphins swam in agitated circles, and the triggerfish darted back and forth. Seeing nothing that might harm him, he tried to locate the net, but the way the sunbeams sliced through the water, he couldn't make it out. "Okay, I'm going in."

Jack handed him the weight belt, and he wrapped in around his waist. Sitting on the platform, he put the fins over his booted feet then scooted back into the BC jacket and buckled it.

"I'm going to check our position. See if we're drifting," said Jack.

Peter fitted the regulator's primary second stage mouthpiece between his lips and gave the captain the okay sign with his fingers. He checked air pressure on the regulator's gauge then slipped sideways into the ocean.

Serenity. Peace. Only the slap of waves on the boat's metal hull cut through the silence. He loved the first three seconds after submerging, the way it seemed as if the world fell away. But he had a mission.

The dolphins wouldn't let him forget it, either. One nudged him on the back and another nosed against his hand. It unnerved him. He reminded himself they didn't attack. He hoped, anyway. Sucking air through the regulator, he adjusted his flotation and began to sink.

The dolphins clicked wildly at him. Come! Come! they cried, diving deeply then racing back to him.

The net came into sight, the top outer edges waving in the current only about twenty-five feet from the bottom of the boat. A scallop net, used to dredge scallops from the ocean floor. He figured it got caught on the wreck and tore from its trawler. Dangerous rigging hung into the depths, probably suspended hundreds of feet down. He let air out of his BC jacket more slowly. Bubbles gurgled past his head on their way to the surface. Sending his gaze over the net, he searched for anything unusual.

The dolphins continued to dip and bob. Below his fins, a pale dot moved back and forth, making him think of the dot on the old Pong video game. The triggerfish. Closer and closer, his heart knocked against his ribs. Straining to make sense of the mess of net, he bent forward. He had to go carefully not to get caught in it himself. He pulled his dive knife free from its calf sheath.

A black, inky mass spread through the water at the net where the triggerfish swam. An octopus? Why in the world would the dolphins get so upset over an octopus caught in a net? Staring, he realized the mass didn't dissipate. It shifted and changed shape with the moving water, but didn't grow larger. Hair!

Oh, God! He jerked and resisted the urge to plummet. Squeezing his nostrils and gently blowing, he cleared his ears, feeling tiny bubbles pass out of his ear canals. He continued his descent, and when his fin brushed the topmost tendrils of hair, a dolphin shot forward and bumped the net.

The hair eased away from the swaying grid and revealed a pale face, a neck, a torso falling backward. Peter thought he would vomit. A woman! With no dive gear! He swallowed hard. It made no sense. What happened to her equipment? How had she lasted so long through the night and into the morning? And at that depth? The wreck had to be in six hundred feet of water. He couldn't wrap his brain around it.

The dolphin darted past, knocking her arm. Her hand flexed and her head turned, but she didn't open her lids. Shit! Adrenaline gave him a jolt.

Level with her, he took his extra second stage and pressed it to her mouth. She struggled weakly, shoving at it, but he forced it between her lips. She didn't draw on it, so he nudged her in the ribs. She had so much hair it seemed to flow everywhere. Brushing some aside, he held her nostrils closed and nudged her again. A hiss of air passed through the mouthpiece.

She heaved with a violent spasm, her eyes flying open and her arms waving through the water. He couldn't believe it! She seemed to cough, sending a riotous mass of bubbles from the regulator into the water between them. She tried to pull it out of her mouth, but he nudged her in the ribs again, and she sucked air.

An arm caught the hair covering her chest, shoving it aside and revealing her naked breasts. He stopped breathing at the sight. Letting go of her mouthpiece, he groped for the net, seeking to keep it from engulfing him as he came to her side. She surprised him by not ripping the mouthpiece free. More air hissed through it as her chest expanded with the inhalation.

Tearing his gaze away from her stunning breasts, he found her staring at him with the most amazing aquamarine eyes. The triggerfish hovered at her shoulder, and the dolphins clicked and clacked as they swam in calm patterns behind her. For a moment, the world stopped spinning. Nothing mattered. Only she and her *friends* existed with him.

Then her eyes rolled back in her head, and she went limp. Peter nudged her in the ribs with the handle of his knife, but she didn't respond. At the same time, the triggerfish butted her neck to no avail. The dolphins flew into a frenzy.

Peter swam around behind her and grasped her under the arms. He tugged and tugged, but she didn't come away from the net. Releasing air from his buoyancy compensator jacket, he sank lower and planted a foot on the anchor where it snagged the bottom of the net. He found an enormous fish caught there. Was she somehow attached to the fish? Perhaps it tried to swallow one of her legs? Or maybe a fishing line connected them?

He followed the glittering tail, unlike anything he'd ever seen, and came immediately to the soft skin of her waist. As though burned, he let her go with a start. Flutter kicking, he backed away. His eyes confirmed the word in his mind. The word that went against everything he understood of undersea life. The word that contradicted reality.

Mermaid!

Chapter Three

A dolphin rammed him, slamming him into the net and yanking the extra second stage from the mermaid's mouth. The net wrapped around him. Peter put up his hands to stave off another attack while slicing the blade through the mesh to keep his equipment from getting bound. Blinking, he wondered if he saw correctly. He cleared his mask, and as he bent his head to blow water from the top, he saw a trickle of blood float out from her tail. Below, two large gray shapes circled. Sharks.

Damn it! Swimming through the hole he had cut, he grabbed her shoulder. Could she be drowning, like sharks and dolphins did when caught in a fishing net? He didn't want to take the chance. He pressed the extra regulator back into her mouth then followed her tail to the crisscross of cords. Two of her side fins appeared sliced by the net and wrapped around loose bits of filament. He grabbed hold of the cords then cut her free.

The sharks didn't follow as he pulled her to the boat. Kicking with all his might, he breathed hard in his exertion to get her to safety as soon as possible. On either side, dolphins swam, squealing *Yes! Yes!*

As he approached the dive platform from underneath, a metallic clanging told him the captain banged something on deck. He gripped the ledge. Pulling upward, he emerged in time to hear the captain's pounding feet head toward the engine room. Perfect timing! He didn't trust Jack Serfass, and didn't want him seeing what he'd brought back.

In a second, he inflated his BC jacket to full capacity and used the counter weight of his tank to lift the mermaid onto the platform. He eased the regulator from her mouth then removed his. Placing a hand on her belly, he felt her breathe while unfastening his BC. He let it float free before pushing it to the platform and shoving it against the transom. He lowered his mask so it hung around his neck and took off his fins. With a grunt, he climbed up. He made sure Jack remained out of sight then checked the mermaid.

She lay unconscious. She was breathing, but he'd never seen anyone so white. It scared him. He set the fins inside the transom, set the tank and BC next to them and piled his weight belt on the deck. Gathering the mermaid in his arms, he glanced over his shoulder. The three dolphins tread water in a line two feet off the dive platform and bobbed their heads. The triggerfish swam back and forth. It looked worried. For a fish.

He shook his head. He was losing his mind.

Surprised she didn't weigh more with such a massive tail, he hiked over the transom and carried her to his stateroom. He laid her on the bed and covered her with a towel from his bag. Running to the lab, he kept an ear out for Jack. A few bangs from the lower level told him the captain still worked on the motor.

He took one of two first aid kits off the lab wall and rushed back to his room. On the bed, she stirred and moaned. He took it as a good sign and locked the door.

At her side, he shook her shoulder. "*Wecken Sie, bitte.*"

She opened her eyes. Such a wonderful blue-green hue, they almost glowed, they were so bright. And surrounded by long, shiny black lashes.

Good. She spoke German. "*Wie sind Sie?*" he asked.

She gave him a blank look.

"*Sprechen Sie Deutsch?*"

Nothing. Just a stare.

"*Habla español?*"

Still nothing. He wished he had time to run the recording through the computer's filter.

"*Francais?*"

She blinked but said nothing. He couldn't take his eyes off her features, so delicate and fine she could pass for a fairy.

He chuckled and shook his head. "*Aegri somnia.*"

"A sick man's dreams?" she asked in English.

"English!" He smacked his forehead. "I'm an idiot."

"I'm frightened. I don't feel well." She put a hand to her head. "Lightheaded."

She *did* look alarmingly pale. Peter pulled the pillow out from under her head and slid his hand under the towel. Lifting her tailfin to aid blood to her brain, he gaped as the towel slid away to reveal two legs. Her fin had transformed into feet in his hands.

She screamed.

"Ssshh!" he urged.

She screamed louder, her eyes wide as she took in the limbs.

Footsteps stomped up the stairs from the lower level. "Dr. Bastian?" Jack called.

He clamped a hand over her mouth. "You've got to be quiet," he whispered.

She continued to scream behind his muffling palm.

The captain banged on the door. "Doc? You in there? I thought I heard a woman scream."

"Yeah, I'm in here. I didn't hear anything. It must have been one of the dolphins." *Go away, you asshole.*

The mermaid stopped screaming and sucked a breath through her nostrils. Wiggling free, she gasped as she rolled off the bed. She hit the floor with a thunk.

Oh, Geez! He rushed around to the other side.

"What's going on in there?"

"Nothing! Nothing! I just dropped..." What? His mind went blank.

"I'm coming in there!" Jack threatened. The latch jiggled.

"Why? You like seeing men naked? I just got out of the shower." Sweat broke out on his forehead, so he unzipped his wetsuit to his bellybutton.

"Damn it, Dr. Bastian. I don't have time for this. The engine's all fucked up. I can't even get juice from the batteries to power the winch."

"Then go fix it." He gathered the squirming mermaid back in his arms and set her on the bed. "Hush!" he hissed.

"You sure everything's okay in there?"

"Jack, for God's sake!"

"Fine, fine. I'll leave you alone. We might be stuck out here for a little while. Just wanted to let you know. But that net's still attached to the wreck somehow, so the anchor has us secured. We might need to call a tow, so it's good we're not drifting."

"Okay. Thanks." Peter put a finger to the mermaid's lips, his eyes on the door, and listened to the captain tromp away.

Suddenly, her lips parted, and she drew his finger into her mouth. He snapped his attention back to her, transfixed as she gently sucked.

* * * *

Ayprial couldn't think straight. She didn't feel like herself. When she got caught the night before, she thought she would die. Then this strange creature freed her. He had taken her to the surface for the first time in her life, and she missed it! *Aaaah!*

She didn't know what he was. He looked half mer, with lower limbs instead of a tail. He spoke like the mer. Some of his words had sounded strange, and she didn't understand. But then he spoke the ancient tongue. And when she used her own, modern language, he'd understood and used it to communicate with her.

He had done something magical to her. She didn't know how, but somehow, he'd turned her tail into limbs like his. She didn't want this! She didn't want them. She needed to get out of this place and back into the ocean.

The lightheadedness continued, and sensations coursed through her like she'd never experienced before. Sensations that warmed her and created longings. When he touched his finger to her lips, she couldn't control her impulse. She sucked on it even as she wondered why she did such a thing. It had to be her maturing. Today, she celebrated her twenty-second birthday. Other mermaids married on this day of their lives, but she had never sought her mate. Was this the price she paid for not listening to Rysha?

The look he gave her made her want more. She had thought his black skin strange. And she didn't like the way it smelled, either. But when he opened it down the middle, it revealed a much more appealing surface underneath. Now, she had to touch it. She ran fingertips along the firm skin, liking his hardness. His strength. His heat.

The sensations grew. Her skin became more sensitive. Between her new limbs, an unfamiliar pressure pounded.

"You're naked," he said, as if realizing it for the first time. His gaze raked her body, making tiny bumps rise on her arms and increasing the longing.

She let him pull his finger free from her lips. "I don't know that word." Squeezing her limbs together, she tried to lessen the uncomfortable throb.

"Naked?" He sighed and sank to his knees. "It means you have no clothes."

Rolling to her side, she caressed his jaw. "That's another word I don't know."

"Clothes? It's what we wear to cover our skin." His lids lowered a little. "Am I imagining you? You're so beautiful."

"If you're imagining me then I'm imagining you, too. I've never seen eyes your color. What are you?" Drinking in his angular features, his eyes the color of the ocean in the light from a blue coral, his short hair reminding her of the soft, brown ocean floor, she couldn't stop stroking him. She ran a hand down the thick cords along his neck and bumped into the edge of his black skin.

He took her hand off his neck. "You have to stop touching me like that. I'm a human."

She tested the word on her tongue. "Human."

"My name is Peter." He set a white box with red markings next to her. "And you're hurt. What's your name?"

"Ayprial."

He touched a finger to her limb. It stung, and she gasped.

"Sorry." He opened the box. "That's an unusual name. It's pretty. It suits you."

Rising up on an elbow, she looked where he had touched. A long red gash oozed blood. Suddenly, the room began to darken.

"Stay with me, Ayprial." He eased her hand from under her head and lowered her to the soft material. "Don't pass out."

"I'm okay," she breathed, not sure how much truth she could claim in the declaration. "Where's Pentri?"

"Just take slow, deep breaths. What's a pentri?"

"I'm not used to breathing air. Pentri's my pet triggerfish." She concentrated on doing as he instructed.

He tore open a white square, filling the air with a sharp, unpleasant odor. "This is going to sting." He swiped something across her injury. "I saw a triggerfish swimming with the dolphins. It might still be around the boat somewhere."

Pain sliced through her limb, like the sting of an urchin, and she trembled. She sucked air between her teeth.

"That's the worst of it." He smiled gently. Taking a larger white square out of the box, he tore it open, too. This one had no odor whatsoever.

"What's that?"

"A bandage. It'll keep the wound clean." He placed it over the gash. "Does it still hurt?"

"A little." The longing washed over her, stronger than ever, and she ran fingers through his hair, just above his delectable ear. She wanted to nibble on that lobe.

"Really, you've got to stop touching me like that. And don't look at me that way, either." His voice sounded strained.

"You don't like it?" She couldn't hide disappointment in her tone.

"I like it too much. Now, roll over so I can clean and bandage your other wound."

She landed her gaze on his lips. Warmth swept through her, making her shudder.

"Are you cold?" He looked at her. Caught her staring at his mouth.

For the life of her, she couldn't stop. She wanted that mouth. How, she wasn't sure. She just wanted it.

As if reading her mind, he leaned in and touched his lips to hers. Yes! Oh, so sweet. Liquid desire filled her chest and spilled low into her belly. He pressed, deepening the contact, and she met him with equal effort.

He smelled sweet, despite the stinky black skin. Up against his face, her nostrils detected the salty sea and a spice that made her mouth water. Wanting to taste him, she touched the tip of her tongue to the crease of his lips.

He snapped backward, his expression heavy and meaningful. "You drive me crazy!"

"Is that a good thing?" she asked, barely recognizing her husky voice.

Chapter Four

She was so hot *he* sweated. Working on catching his breath, Peter pulled his wetsuit off his shoulders and peeled off the arms, flipping them inside out in the process. With the greatest effort he'd ever put into anything, he averted his gaze from her incredible, heart-stopping curves.

Her eyes popped. "How did you do that?" She appeared appalled.

"Do what?"

"Remove your skin!"

He laughed. He couldn't help it. "This isn't skin." He slid a thumb under the neoprene and gave it a snap against his abdomen. "This is a wetsuit. It keeps me warm when I dive."

Her feminine, arched brows closed in on one another above the bridge of her pert nose. "The water makes you cold?"

With his cock straining against the unforgiving neoprene, he could use some cold water slaking down his overheated body. "Yeah. Now please roll over so I can care for your other wound."

When she did, he bit back a groan. She had the tastiest ass! He fought the urge to sink his teeth into it.

Turning his back, he planted his fists on his hips and took a deep breath. He closed his eyes and got control. When he faced her once again, she looked at him over her shoulder. He could do this.

Working quickly, he swabbed the second laceration, hating her hiss of pain, and secured an adhesive bandage over the weeping injury. Sweat beaded his forehead, chest and shoulders. He had to get out of the wetsuit. "Go ahead and get under the covers," he said.

Ayprial shot him a perplexed glance. "Covers?"

"You're laying on them." He pointed at the head of the bed where the top of the blanket met the edge of the mattress.

"Will you join me?" As soon as the words left her lips, she looked surprised that she said them.

His knees went weak. "Uh…no. Look, could you please just cover yourself?"

Her face fell. "I'm unattractive to you."

"God, no!" In a single step, he reached her side and sat at her hip. He hooked a fingertip on a wet tress clinging to her forehead and smoothed it into the ebony hair at her temple. "You're about the loveliest woman I've ever met."

"I'm not a woman. I'm just a mer." Her eyes went liquid, baring her insecurity.

"Sweetheart, you're more woman than some of the human women I've known. Mer or not."

Her gaze slid away, and he snuck a peek at her luscious breasts. A mistake. His dick sprang, begging to slide between those white, coral-peaked globes. If she weren't a mermaid, he'd suspect she had a boob-job, they looked so firm and round.

"I'm afraid," she whispered.

He gathered her close, hugging her and gaining a rush from the protectiveness she elicited in him. "You're safe with me."

"I'm alone," she whispered. "I've always been alone, even with other mer around."

Though he couldn't relate, having a loving family, close friends, and co-workers he truly enjoyed working with, his heart went out to her. "Well, you're not alone right now."

"You care about me?" Her voice, so small and shy, touched him deeply.

"Yeah. I do." He couldn't say why if she asked, but he did. He cared.

"I've never been hugged."

Well, that was just tragic. "You have now." He squeezed her a bit tighter then lowered her back to the mattress. He slid aside the covers. Hooking a hand behind her knees, he swung her legs onto the fitted sheet and pulled the top sheet and blanket over her. A tear seeped from the corner of her eye, but she didn't seem to notice. "Are you okay?" he asked.

"I'm tired," she said with a sigh.

"Then get some rest. If you're okay here for a little while, I need to go do some work. I won't be long." He bent and unzipped his boots. After kicking them off, he stripped the wetsuit from his legs and tossed it toward the door.

"You're leaving?"

"No, I'll be down the hall in my lab. If you call, I'll hear you and come. I promise." He needed to get those numbers loaded and transmitted. He had no idea what to do with this unexpected development. One thing was certain, though. He needed to get away from her so he could think clearly.

In his lab, he spent five minutes deleting the night data from sensor *number three* so Ben wouldn't find out about Ayprial before Peter could tell him. He downloaded the recordings from *number one* and *number two*. While transferring data from *number four*, the captain tried to start the boat's engine. It whirred and whined but didn't start.

Down the hall, he heard a faint, high-pitched keening. Damn it. He needed two more minutes.

Ignoring Ayprial's call, and knowing Jack couldn't hear it in the engine room or on the bridge, he finished the download. He attached the power booster to a wall adaptor designed to pull electricity directly from the batteries in the engine room, plugged the feeder line into it from the computer, and hit *send*. Done. Now he could go see to the mermaid.

Just thinking about her made his vitals stir. Before he reached his stateroom door, Jack tried to start the engine again. It didn't whir. It didn't whine. It just sort of groaned and gave up with a sputter. Great. He did *not* relish the thought of trying to keep Ayprial hidden from Jack all afternoon.

The keening sounded again, louder this time. He had to quiet her. Flinging open the door, ready to chastise her for making too much noise, he rushed inside and halted in his tracks.

Ayprial lay atop the covers, glistening with perspiration, with her eyes closed and her hand between her legs. Her finger stroked her pussy, and she wailed.

His jaw hit his chest. Realizing he stood with the door open, his palm still on the latch, he swung it closed ,and it banged.

* * * *

Ayprial jerked and pulled her hand out from between her limbs with a guilty start. Peter looked angry. But not. She couldn't quite keep up with the emotions flashing across his features. Then another wave of pleasure-pain took her unawares, and she closed her lids and braced, a cry ripping from her lips.

Peter hurried to her side. "You have to stop that. You're too loud."

The wave subsided, and water slipped down her cheek. "I can't help it," she said. "I think I'm dying."

"Are you in pain? Tell me why you think you're dying." He took her hand in his.

"I can't explain it. I… I…hurt." She squeezed his fingers as the pain started at the base of her torso and shot a bolt deep into her belly. "Aaaa-aa-A!"

"What? What is it?" He sat at her hip and grasped both her shoulders.

"I can't stand this!" she cried when she could speak.

"Where does it hurt?" He looked so concerned.

"Here." She touched a finger to that aching place between her limbs.

"Are you kidding me?"

Another drop of water fell from her eye.

He wiped it away. "You're really hurting, aren't you?"

She nodded. Slipping her finger into the folds, she found some slight relief from the pain. "I don't know what to do. Today is my maturity. I was supposed to find a lifemate, but I didn't. And now I think I'm dying."

His brows furrowed. "A lifemate? Maturity? Are you trying to tell me you're in heat?"

"I don't know what that means!" she bit out as another wave of pain made her tense. "Aaa-aaa-AAAA!"

"Stop! My God, Ayprial. You're going to have Captain Serfass running to break down the door if he hears you."

"I can't—" Her breath hitched. "I can't help it."

"What can I do? What do you need?" He licked his lips.

She wanted his tongue! Like nothing she'd ever wanted before, she wanted that tongue. All over her. She craved it. "Lick me."

"What?" He released her shoulders as if they had turned to slimy algae.

"Please. I beg you. I think it will help. Lick me."

He appeared incredulous and didn't move. She fought the urge to hit him. More water leaking from her eyes, she rocked her head back on crashing pain-pleasure. It took her breath away. When it peaked, she let out another cry.

"Okay! Okay! If it'll make you stop yelling." He stood. "But I've got to get out of this damned swimsuit. You've got me all tied up in knots."

She didn't know what he meant, but she understood he intended to help. Blinking moisture from her eyes, she raised up on elbows. He bent and slid the colorful covering from his hips. When he rose, she couldn't take her gaze from the protruding member pointing at her from a nest of dark curls. Instinct kicked in, and she understood suddenly that he had what she needed.

Chapter Five

Peter took a deep breath. He couldn't deny he had thought of little else since the towel had slid off her shapely legs an hour ago. But to have her beg him to touch her? Again, he had the sense he was in some kind of dream.

Suffering etched her features. He didn't fully comprehend what she endured. Until that afternoon, he'd thought mermaids only a myth. Now, he realized he had a lot to learn. And the first lesson would involve a mermaid's anatomy. Before he reached the bed, he smelled her excitement. Not a fishy odor he would expect from someone who lived in the ocean, but a musky, spicy fragrance that beckoned him. Climbing onto the bed, he took her knees and spread them wide.

She had no hair. Not a single curl hid the delights awaiting him. From her opening, wetness seeped clear and thick. His cock jumped, straining to bathe in those heavy juices then sink into her. But she had asked him to lick her. He had to trust her to know what she needed. So he would lick her.

He sent one last look at her. She begged him with her eyes, so he moved forward and inhaled. Even her scent begged him. Drew him with an almost supernatural pull.

"Spread your legs a little wider, sweetheart," he said.

"Legs?"

He ran fingers from her ankle, up over her bent knee, and down her inner thigh. "Leg."

Her thighs fell, opening the way for him. With a fingertip, he grazed the instep of her foot. "Foot," he said.

"Foot." Her voice sounded husky, needy.

He swallowed. Raking his finger higher, he rasped, "Calf…knee… thigh."

"Mmm. I like the way you touch me," she whispered.

He sent his tongue up the center of her slit. Spicy sweet. Delicious. She moaned. The sound resonated inside him, making him want to answer in kind. Needing to take his mind off his rattling senses, he licked up the outer fold.

"Labia majora," he whispered, puffing air over her flesh. She panted.

He sent the tip of his tongue along the inner petals. "Labia minora."

She bit her lower lip and hummed low.

Finding the bundle of nerves nestled at the top, he said, "Clitoris." He wrapped his lips around it and gave a gentle suck.

She groaned, but not a groan he'd ever heard. It held two tones, harmonious, that thrummed his nerves like a harp. His penis responded instantly, and his hips bucked. What was she doing to him?

He searched frantically for something to think about that would take his mind off his aching need, but he could only think about the fact that he hadn't brought condoms. Why would he need condoms on a research boat with only Jack Serfass for company? Damn it. He gave her clit a lick and another suck, and she rose to meet his gaze. Her pupils expanded, nearly swallowing the aqua color of her irises, and she issued a beautiful three-note tune that had him on his knees and poised. His mind said *no*, but his body moved of its own accord. With a tremendous effort, he hiked a leg over hers, making penetration impossible. He slid along her soft, smooth skin until he met her face-to-face.

"Please," she pleaded.

"Too fast. It's too fast." He lowered his lips to hers.

The moment their mouths touched, he stopped thinking of her as an animal, a creature he found caught in a net. Her arms came around his back. The arms of a woman. Her lips moved against his. The lips of a woman. Her body arched against him. The body of a woman. Oh, God. His entire being vibrated with need. Her lips parted, and he dipped in for a taste. Sweet. Rich. A surprising caramel flavor he hadn't expected. She opened fully, and he explored, enjoying the touch and glide of her tongue against his.

He closed his eyes, but suddenly saw stars as her knee contacted with his groin. He jerked and reached for his screaming balls.

"I'm so sorry!" she cried.

He squeezed his eyes closed against the breath-stealing stabs.

"I'm not used to these limbs. Legs," she corrected herself.

Something felt strange. He peeked a look and saw his cock still stood at attention. With a blow like that, it should've shrunk and tried to hide. Upright on his knees, he gazed down her.

With a small, apologetic smile, she sat and reached for his loins. He held out a hand. "Don't."

"But I can help."

Interested to see what she would do, and not believing it could hurt any more than it already did, he let her slip her fingers between his thighs. She cupped his testicles and made a low humming sound. The pain disappeared.

Amazed, he could only stare as she ran her fingers along his sack then grasped his cock. Yes! Her hand was heaven.

"I want this. Inside me," she said.

He did, too. More than he could say. "I don't have protection."

"I won't bite," she said, her serious expression making him swallow a laugh.

"No, but you've got a pretty mean knee." Peter tapped a palm on one.

Her face drooped into a moue. "I said I was sorry."

He smiled to let her know he held no enmity. "I forgive you. Now, where were we?"

"Your mouth played with mine. And I liked it very much, but I'd rather have that inside me." She pointed at his rod.

"We can't." Man, it actually hurt to say that!

"But I have pain." She cupped her pussy and gazed at him with huge, gorgeous eyes. "I need it."

Well, when you put it like that...Wait a minute! He shook his head, trying to clear it. Did she cast some kind of mer-spell on him? "How about if I lick you some more?"

"That helped, but it didn't make the ache go away."

"Ache?" The same ache that drove him crazy at the moment?

"Please?" she whispered.

He moved to lie next to her, but at the same time, she lifted an arm to brush her thick, black hair off a slender shoulder and caught him in the eye with her elbow. "Ow!" he wailed, slapping a hand on the smarting brow bone.

"Oh! Peter, I'm so sorry!" She sniffed.

He looked at her through his good eye. Was she going to cry? *Don't cry. I can't handle it when women cry.*

"I'll get the white box." She shifted to the edge of the bed. With a squeal, and arms and legs flailing wildly, she teetered over the edge. "Oof!"

"Ayprial? Are you okay?" He peeped over then set a foot on the floor.

"Ow! You're on my hair," she cried, falling back.

A chuckle gurgled out of him against his will.

"This isn't funny," she accused, sitting and scowling.

She looked so adorable, and beautiful, and sexy, and well, *funny* sitting on the floor in a heap of awkward knees and ankles and feet. He couldn't stop a guffaw.

Her cheeks growing pink, she grasped his wrist and pulled him off the mattress. He landed beside her. "Oof!"

"There. Now you know how I feel."

Passion rushed him unawares, and he eased her to her back on the carpet. Capturing her mouth, he urged her to open while sending his hands over her. Long, strong arms with delicate, tapered fingers. A swan's neck. Collar bones covered in luxurious satin. High, firm breasts a tad too large to fit perfectly in his hands. Skin like velvet over her tight waist.

Letting go of her mouth, he rained kisses down her throat. "Now…I…know…how…you…feel." He captured a hard nipple and sucked. She gasped, a sound that echoed delightfully in his head. Gently, he grazed it with his teeth, making her gasp again.

He sent his fingers lower, into her slit. So wet. So warm. Stroking her, he loved the way she arched and writhed, breathing heavily. He kissed lower, along the muscular dip at the center of her abdomen, and urged her thighs apart with his hand. She complied readily, her responses to his kisses and caresses immediate and eager. She made that harmonious trill that brought him to maximum, painful erection. He couldn't stop himself, this time. Working his way between her thighs, he rested his pelvis against her.

"Yes," she said with a sigh.

She wanted this as much as he did. Protection be damned, he needed her. Now!

Chapter Six

Ayprial trembled, her body crying out to him. He smelled so good. Hugging him closer, she rose to taste him, laving his throat and loving the salty, spicy taste of his skin. He moaned.

She wrapped her lower legs behind his bent knees and flexed, bringing his jutting limb to the apex where her need tortured her. When Peter touched the tip of it to her opening, she shuddered. Now, she silently implored.

Shifting, he eased into her. The pressure provided instant relief. Sighing, she tipped her head to rest on the floor. She spread her knees wider and tilted her hips to draw him in deeper. So hard. So slick. She wanted all of him.

"More," she said, relaxing her neck to look at him.

His skin stretched taut over his cheekbones, and his eyes dark and stormy, he said with a tight voice, "I don't want to hurt you."

It hurt for him *not* to! Didn't he understand that? Waves lapped at the boat's hull, slapping it with a rhythm that hinted at something carnal. Something ancient. "Please. More."

He closed his eyes and threw back his head. His mouth opened on a silent cry as he thrust fully into her.

A bolt of sheer, electric pleasure ripped through her. "Yes!" she exclaimed, the agony gone in an instant.

He filled her completely. Her walls gripped him, sending waves of undulating rapture deep into her belly. Gasping, she stared as his face contorted into a series of expressions that matched her every emotion. Her heart leapt with joy when his eyes met hers. She read passion, caring and intelligence there. She wanted him. Heart and soul, she wanted him for her own.

Then he withdrew and thrust again. All thought fled as her body arched in pure reaction. He pumped again and again. Coming to pieces, bit by bit, she hugged her legs around his back, gaining strength from his stamina.

A new ache began. Not a painful one like the earlier throbbing that had threatened to drive her mad, but a current of rushing ecstasy that promised something elusive and wonderful. She strained for it. Meeting him thrust for pounding thrust, she tensed as every muscle in her body flexed.

She tilted her hips as far as she could, and he touched a spot at the heart of her core. A sweet spot that made her want to cry out with each driving penetration.

The current became a crashing wave that slammed her into bliss. She gasped, her senses toppling. End over end, she spun into a fathomless abyss of utter sensation and release.

Slowly coming back to her senses, she grasped his shoulders. He continued to work toward his own release, his features twisted into a mask of pleasurable agony. She'd never seen such a look, but she understood it.

His eyes glazed and his body hard with the tension of his effort, he lowered his lips to hers. She opened. Welcomed his tongue inside. Feasted on him. He tasted foreign, exotic.

Keeping time with him, she felt her body grip him inside. He groaned and buried his face in her shoulder. Hugging him close, she closed her lids and inhaled as he thrust so deeply it made her jerk in surprise. His body bucked and shivered, his seated member doing something that caused bursts of liquid heat to wash through her.

As he began to relax, she pressed soft kisses to his hair, his ear, his cheek. He peppered her shoulder and throat with the same. Her heart ached now. And sadness seeped into her soul. Refusing to explore it, or give in to it, she hardened her resolve. She wanted him. No, she needed Peter. Human or not, he was her lifemate.

"Feel better?" he asked, settling to the floor beside her.

With a great sigh, she said, "Very."

"That was incredible." He smiled, his voice low and lazy.

She nodded. "The most incredible thing I've ever felt."

Rising on an elbow and resting his cheek against his palm, he gazed on her. He combed away hair stuck to perspiration along her cheek. "This floor is hard. Let's get on the bed."

Her stomach flip-flopped. "And do it again?"

He grinned then laughed. "As much as I'd love to, I don't think that's a good idea." He stood and offered her a hand.

"Why not?" She slid her fingers along his proffered palm and sat. Unsure what to do next, she sent him a questioning look.

"Bend your knees and push with your legs."

He tugged gently as she followed his instruction. Wobbling to a stand, she grabbed his shoulder. "This doesn't feel right."

"You're doing fine," he reassured. "Take a step."

Ayprial lifted a foot then planted it on the floor, closer to the bed, but her hip went one way while her shoulders went another. Swinging her free arm in an attempt to gain some balance, she tipped backward and smacked him in the forehead with the back of her flailing hand.

He gripped her arm tighter and pushed her upright. "That hurt."

"Sorry," she said in a small voice. "It's much easier in the water."

"That's true. But don't give up. Once you get the hang of moving around, you'll wonder why you ever had a problem."

She smiled.

"Go ahead and take another step." He put a hand on her waist and held her steady.

She did as he instructed, making sure to keep her hips and shoulders in line. It worked! She beamed as he helped her turn and sit.

Peter went to a cloth container and pulled out some gray material. "Here," he said, handing it over. "Put it on."

"What is it?" She turned it this way and that, but couldn't figure how to work it.

"It's a T-shirt." He bent to a pile of more material on the floor and picked out a small white piece. Holding it low, he put his feet through some holes and pulled it over his hips.

Studying the thing in her hands, she found holes in it, too. So she bent over her knees and lifted a foot to insert into the T-shirt.

"No, no." He chuckled. "Here, I'll help you." He pulled material over his head that looked similar to what she held. Then, kneeling before her, he helped her pull the gray T-shirt over her head and poke her arms through the holes.

Weird. But strangely comfortable. She rubbed a hand over the front where it covered her chest. "It's so soft. As soft as warm water."

He smiled and stretched out on the bed behind her. "Come here." Holding out his arms, he waggled his fingers.

She lifted her legs onto the bed and settled into his waiting embrace. Lying against him, with her cheek on his chest and one knee resting atop his leg, she felt graceful for the first time since leaving the ocean. She loved how their curves fit so perfectly.

"You have the most beautiful hair I've ever seen." He combed his fingers through it. "It was pretty in the water, but now that it's dry, it's so wavy and shiny."

His fingertips along her scalp relaxed and soothed her. "Thank you. It's never been dry before. For that matter, *I've* never been dry before. I rather like it. And thank you for rescuing me." She glanced at him, but he stared at the ceiling, so she settled again.

"How did you get caught in the net?"

From below, farther back in the boat, a deep rumble shook the bed. "What was that?"

"Captain Serfass is trying to get the engine started."

"Engine?"

"Yeah, it's the machine that makes the boat go."

"I understand. And when he gets it working, you'll leave? Go back to land?" Her heart broke at the thought.

"Yes. It's where I live. Now, back to the subject. The net?"

"Oh, yes. I was on my way to Stryka. I didn't see it and ran right into it. I would've been fine if I'd just backed away, but I turned while I was still up against it, and those strings cut me. I got caught and couldn't get out. It was too dark." Poor Pentri had swum circles in a panic for hours. She shook her head at her own stupidity.

"Your side tailfins wrapped around the filaments. You were probably too weak by morning to see it and work yourself free." His stroking fingers went lower, rubbing ovals over her back.

"I was drowning."

"I know. We see it all the time with sharks and dolphins." He huffed, a sound that reassured her.

She rubbed her cheek on his soft shirt and eased her arm across his stomach. His muscles tensed, his hard strength instilling a sense of security, and she sighed with contentment. "How did you know I was there?"

"I'm a scientist. I came out here today to retrieve our sensors. I'm doing a study on whale song, trying to link their communication to a language we can translate and understand."

A thrill ran through her. "You study creatures in the ocean?"

"Yeah. That's what I do for a living. I love it. Sometimes it's frustrating, but sometimes it's really exciting."

Her heart skipped a beat with excitement. A scientist! She didn't know a whole lot about her world, but she could help him in his work with ocean languages. And he surely had a great deal to teach her. Together, they could learn so much more. Rolling, she stretched out atop him and crossed her hands on his chest. His eyes appeared lighter now. More cheerful and bright. His words tapped into her lifetime of longing and curiosity.

"I can't believe you study the ocean. I've always wanted to do that!" Did she sound too eager? Suddenly, she didn't care. She'd found someone who shared her greatest interest.

He chuckled. "You've wanted to study the ocean? But you live in it. Don't you have a complete understanding?"

"No. Do you have a complete understanding of life on land?"

"Good point. No, I don't. I'm sure I understand it better than you, who've never been there. But I don't know everything about it." He ran fingers of both hands through her hair, pushing it away from her face. With a thoughtful tilt of his head, he narrowed his eyes and said, "How did those dolphins know I wouldn't hurt you?"

"What dolphins?"

"When I arrived this morning to retrieve my sensors, they came and tried to lead me to you. I should've listened. But I didn't come back for you until I heard you on a sensor recording." He shook his head. "You could've died."

Her heart went out to him. She loved his concern. "But I didn't. Don't be so unforgiving of yourself." She kissed the tip of his nose, relieved when he smiled. "I don't remember dolphins. They probably responded to my cries for help but didn't arrive before I blacked out. To be honest, I'm surprised sharks didn't hear my cries and come for the feast."

"They came," he said, his voice low and serious.

Her stomach twisted in her gut and she swallowed. "You came in after me with sharks threatening?"

"They followed the net up when we pulled it near the surface and were circling below. I didn't see them until I was freeing your tail. But I still don't understand how the dolphins could know I would help."

He shifted his hips under hers, and an itch of longing sliced through her slit. "Dolphins read the electrical charge that comes off of us. They know our intent, our mood, our needs." Needs. Oh, how she suddenly had a need!

"Electrical charges. That's fascinating!" His eyes lit up. "How do they read them? Do they see them? Feel them? Smell them?"

"I don't know. But I want to. And so much more." The itch grew into pinpricks of swelling that begged for some relief. Wrapping her hands behind his neck, she placed a kiss on his chin then his jaw. She worked down to the side of his neck, pecking and sucking along the length. She hooked a finger under his neckline and moved the material aside.

His breathing grew more labored, and his fingers found the bottom edge of her shirt. Caressing her back at the edge of the material, he hissed in a breath through his teeth when she nibbled his collarbone. He sent his hands lower. "You've got a great ass," he whispered, and squeezed the mounds.

Moisture rushed out and coated the now pulsing folds of her pussy. Grinding against him, she gave his earlobe a lick and whispered, "I want you inside me again."

"I can't. I shouldn't have the first time." He groaned, grasped her by the waist and lifted her off him. Catapulting from the bed, he stood with his back to her for a moment and ran his fingers through his hair. When he turned, the proof of his own need pressed against the white fabric encasing his hips.

"Why?" Did he reject her? Would he send her back to the sea and never want to see her again?

"Because it's wrong. And because we don't know enough about the consequences we might face. Might already face." In two wide strides, he reached his cloth container and pulled out another garment. He put his feet into this one, too, and secured it around his hips.

Two layers of material around his hips? Humans were strange. "But what if I can't control it? Like last time. What if I start hurting? I don't want to get you in trouble." She grazed a fingernail over the bandage on her right thigh and used the resulting pain to dampen the growing ache between her legs.

"Just do your best. I've got something I have to do. I'll be back in about ten minutes."

Chapter Seven

Peter checked the computer screen and found a message confirming the information had been successfully transferred to the research facility's main database. The screen dimmed, so he reached over to the wall and flicked a switch that rerouted power from the main engine to a bank of backup batteries in the lab. When the screen instantly grew bright, he plugged an adaptor into the lab's satellite phone and jacked it directly into the power booster. He dialed Ben's number and listened to clicks and clunks as his signal passed through the booster, through the satellite receiving station, and connected to a land phone line. Finally, Ben's phone rang.

"Hello?" Peter's assistant sounded hoarse.

"Hey. It's Peter. How're you feeling?"

"Hi, Doc. I feel like hell. But I have the information you sent. It should only take a little while to chart the recordings." Ben succumbed to a bout of coughing.

"Geez, aren't you taking something for that?" Peter wondered if he should've called his sister instead. He heard the captain talking, but the closed lab door muffled the sound, and he couldn't make out what the man griped about this time. He shrugged and listened to Ben.

"I ran to the drugstore this morning and picked up cough and cold medicine, but I haven't taken any yet."

"Why not?"

"I don't want to take it on an empty stomach. I'm heating lunch right now. Then I'll take it." He coughed again. "You sound different. Everything okay?"

Peter took a deep breath and slowly let it out. "I've made a discovery. Something I rescued from a scallop net caught on a wreck."

"What is it?" Ben asked with excitement. "Are you bringing it back?"

"I don't know yet. Besides, we're broken down. Serfass has been trying to get the engine going for an hour."

"You want me to call for a tow?"

"Not yet. I'll call again in a while."

Ben sniffled. "Don't wait too long. Talk to you later."

Peter ended the call, put the phone in its holder and shut down the power booster. Trying to keep the sexy mermaid from his thoughts, he worked at packing the sensors and archiving the information. Having such a delicious temptation only two doors away made it difficult to concentrate. So he worked faster.

* * * *

Ayprial sighed and hoped he would return quickly. With the prospect of Peter heading back to land that day, she had some decisions to make. And they needed time to talk. She knew what she wanted. Him. But if he didn't want her in return, she wouldn't force herself on him. She'd go back to the ocean and continue to Stryka. It would break her heart, but she'd do it.

A knock on the door made her jump.

"Dr. Bastian? The batteries are drained. Do you have your lab equipment pulling power from the engine room?"

Captain Serfass. Peter didn't want him to know about her. She held her silence.

"Dr Bastian? You in there?"

She swung her legs over the side of the bed and stood. Peter's T-shirt hung on her to mid-thigh, and she was glad for the warmth and cover it provided. With a hand on the wall, she focused on walking. If he agreed to take her home with him, she'd need the skill.

More knocking. "Hey! I'm talking to you!"

Suddenly the door flew open. Ayprial nearly buckled under the surprise, but she locked her knees and leaned into the wall. In the doorway stood an older man with a scruff of red hair smattering his jaw. He wore a hat with a bill that shaded beady, milky gray eyes. Eyes that took her in from head to toe and made her want to brush away his gaze.

"What do we have here?" he asked, taking a step into the room. His hard lips cracked to reveal yellow teeth. He pulled a red cloth from the garment covering his hips and legs and wiped his grimy hands. It didn't help. When he tucked it back away, his fingertips were still black. "So *you're* what the doctor was doing in here. When did he sneak you on board?"

She shook her head, taking an instant dislike to this human.

He took another step and narrowed his eyes. "You look familiar." He scratched his head and left a patch of black on the side of his hat. "Like a bad dream," he drawled. Looking down at his feet, he said in a low, deadly tone, "A bad dream." His head snapped up and anger shot from his stare. "That wasn't a bad dream. I saw you!" He pointed a nasty finger at her and took another step.

Ayprial flattened her back to the wall, not sure where to go but sensing she needed to get away from this man.

"In the ocean. With a man and a baby. I saw you right before my father hit you with his boat. What were you doing in the middle of the ocean like that? You just showed up out of nowhere." He shook his head and fisted his hand on his side. "But that was twenty years ago. You haven't changed at all!" His voice pitched on a hysterical note. "I thought I imagined it. Am I imagining you? Or are you a ghost?"

She took a sliding step along the wall. "I don't know," she whispered. "I don't know what you're talking about." Where was Peter?

"We heard the impact. The boat lurched. I remember," he said, pointing at her again. "I almost went over the side. I tried to tell my dad I saw you three in the water before he hit you, but he wouldn't believe me. Said we probably just hit a sea turtle or something. He didn't think of me as a man, even though I was getting ready to graduate from high school."

"I-I don't know what you're talking about." But she did. Or, at least, she began to wonder. Was that how her parents died? Under a boat driven by this man's father?

"I know your face," he insisted. "I've seen it in my dreams nearly every night since that accident. Why did I ever let my father convince me I only imagined you?"

Not Ayprial. Her mother. She shook her head and took another step away.

He grabbed her arm. "You were there. Where's the man? Where's the baby?"

She didn't dare confirm the truth of what had so clearly become a nightmare to him. When his fingers bit into her arm, she screamed.

"My God." The captain gasped. "Dr. Bastian pulled you out of the ocean, didn't he? He suited up and went in after you. At the fishing net." He bent his head and looked at her legs. "What are you? A siren?"

Peter rushed in. "Get your hand off her!" Grabbing the captain by the shoulder, he turned him and sent his fist into the man's face.

Ayprial almost lost her balance as Captain Serfass crumpled, his grip on her arm threatening to drag her down as he slumped to the floor.

Peter hurried to her side and took her hand. "I heard you scream. Are you okay?"

She nodded, not sure what to say. She let him lead her to the bed then she sat on edge and buried her face in her hands. "He knew things about me. About my family, I mean."

"Jack Serfass knows about your family? I don't understand."

Ayprial worked at drawing air into her lungs as her mind whirled. "I was raised in an orphanage. My parents died when I was a baby. I had no family. No one. I've been so alone all my life until you." She sent him a pleading look, silently begging him to understand and not turn her away. "Then he came in here—"

"I forgot to lock the door. Sorry about that."

She waved a hand, saying, "No, you see, he *knew*. He knew how my parents died. He looked at me but thought he was looking at my mother."

He sat next to her and covered her hands with one of his. "I'm not following."

"My parents brought me to the ocean's surface. But Jack's father hit them with his boat. It was an accident. Jack saw us, but his father didn't."

"Jack Serfass knows you're a mermaid?"

The subject of their conversation groaned and stirred.

"I don't think so." She shook her head. "He said something about a siren?"

Peter laughed. "Yeah, that makes so much more sense than a mermaid. Neither of which exist. Supposedly." He rolled his eyes. "Geez."

"What's going to happen now? Are you going to send me back to the sea?" Saying the words took more effort than she expected.

"I don't know. First, we have to talk to Jack." He went to the floor next to the sprawled captain and shook the man's shoulder. "Wake up, Captain."

"You hit me," Jack said, cupping his cheekbone and pushing to a sitting position.

"Then don't grab people. It's rude." Peter glanced at Ayprial and winked.

She smiled, despite everything.

The captain shot angry barbs at her in his gaze. "She's not what she seems. Trust me."

"Oh, please. What would you know?" Peter stood and offered the downed man a hand.

Jack took it and stood with a grunt, still clutching his face. "She's a sea creature. She could make us rich."

"Knock it off ,or I'll hit you again. Have you lost your mind, Serfass?" Peter let go of the man's hand and looked at the grime left behind. "She's a woman. Beautiful, smart, clumsy. But just a woman. Now how close are you to getting that engine running?"

The captain gave her a wary look. "I'm not. The thing needs an overhaul. I could get her to limp back to shore if I had a patch for the intake valve, but I don't. We're going to need a tow."

"Then let's call for one."

Ayprial couldn't believe how easily Peter had gotten the man's mind off of her. She didn't dare move or speak and call attention to herself.

"Can't," Captain Serfass huffed.

"Why not?"

"The backup battery in the electronics panel up on the bridge is dead. I checked it. Should've checked it before we left shore this morning. Who knows how long it's been since they changed it out for a fresh one." He touched fingertips to the swelling cheekbone and winced. "I need some ice."

Peter gave him a gentle shove toward the door. "Go get some ice from the galley. I'll get a battery from the lab so you can call for a tow on the radio."

Jack disappeared around the corner, and Ayprial leapt to her feet. "I'm not staying in here without you."

Peter took her hand and led her out. "Don't worry about Jack Serfass." He opened a door and took her into a large room full of tables and boxes and wires. "He was in a car accident about three years ago. Drunk driving. His memory's crap. By this time tomorrow, he won't remember how he got that lump on his cheek, much less meeting you. He's okay on a day trip, but I'd never let him captain a boat for a longer trip."

He opened a large white case, revealing a line of black boxes. He unfastened wires from one and lifted it out.

"What is this place?" she asked.

"It's a science lab. I share it with three other scientists and a number of assistants. We learn about the ocean in here." He gave her a reassuring smile then nodded toward the door. "Come on. We'll go up on deck, and you can see if your triggerfish is still around."

With eagerness in her step, she followed him into the sunshine. She'd never seen light so bright and had to squint against the shock. He tucked the box under an arm and climbed to a higher level on the boat, but Ayprial went to the back of the boat and searched for Pentri.

A dolphin poked its head from the water and bobbed at her. "You okay! We worried."

"I'm fine," she said. "Thank you for finding the human."

"Good human. Save you. Yes!"

"Yes. Thank you. He tended my wounds. I'm going to be okay." She slapped the shelf on the boat's side to send a reinforcing signal. "Have you seen Pentri?"

The dolphin smacked the bottom of its bottlenose on the water's surface. "Yes! Yes! Yes! Coming! Coming now."

Another dolphin rose from the gentle waves and grinned at Ayprial. "Good! Saved. Coming home?"

Her pet arrived and hovered at the corner of the platform, keeping an eye on her. She smiled and hopped over. The moment her feet landed in the shallow water sloshing across the platform, they transformed into a fin. With a yelp, she toppled. Her legs became a tail, but she didn't care. Dipping a hand into the water, she stroked the triggerfish. He wiggled with delight.

She turned to the second dolphin. "I don't want to go home. I want to stay with the human." She looked at Pentri. "But I don't want to leave you, either."

"Stay with good human? Lifemate? Love good human?" asked the first dolphin.

"Lifemate, yes." And he was a good human. The best of men, she would guess. But love? Maybe. Just maybe.

Chapter Eight

Peter finished switching out the console battery then turned on the radio. Static welcomed him, so he nodded approval and turned it off. In the silence, he noticed a faint clicking sound. Searching through the console, he sought the source. A thump at the rear of the boat made him spin in time to see Ayprial go down. Damn it!

Unlike Captain Serfass, he didn't trust his dexterity, so he had to descend rung for rung. His heart thudded against his ribs, and his feet hit the deck running for the transom. He didn't want her to go. And to his surprise, his urgency to reach her had less to do with his passion to understand sea life than his passion to understand *her*. She intrigued him. Stirred him. Brought him to life and made him think about the future.

At the stern, he found Ayprial lounging across the dive platform, her tail flicking happily while she "talked" to two dolphins. "Ayprial?" he interrupted.

"Peter! I found Pentri. He was here the whole time, like you said." She smiled at him over her shoulder.

"Yes! Yes!" squealed the first dolphin.

Peter grinned. "Yes," he said and nodded.

"You understand them!" cried Ayprial.

"Only a few words. And I don't speak dolphin, like you clearly do." He couldn't help but be impressed. He could learn so much from her. "Where are your bandages?" he asked, running his gaze along her tail. Her side fins appeared raw, angry and painful, but no longer bleeding.

She glanced down. "They must have come off when my tail formed."

She didn't seem bothered at all that she had her tail back. Was she ready to return to the ocean? Ready to leave him? Why did that bother him so much when he'd only known her a few hours?

A distant, rhythmic knocking carried to them on the salt air. He went to the starboard side and looked out past the bow. A large commercial fishing boat clunked its way toward them from the horizon. With a heavy heart, he joined her and said, "I guess it's time for you to go. We've got company on the way."

Her stunning aqua eyes showed open hurt. He took hope.

"Do you want me to leave?" she asked.

He placed his forearms on the transom and leaned over her. "Not even a little bit."

A slow curl of her lips revealed straight white teeth. "I don't want to go, either."

"Then let's get you out of sight and dried off." He held out his hand.

"I don't want to leave Pentri."

He looked at the triggerfish. "We can't take him."

"Why not?"

"Triggerfish his size don't usually thrive in captivity." He studied Pentri. The fish acted like a dog, wiggling under her caressing fingers and nudging her hand when she stopped. Funny fish.

"He wouldn't be a captive. He'd live with me. That's all he wants." She looked ready to cry.

The clunking trawler grew louder, and Jack's footsteps approached. He would have to time her move to the cabin just right. He glanced over his shoulder. Jack climbed to the bridge. "Fish get stressed when they're transported."

Ayprial touched his outstretched hand. "He'll be happy to be with me. Just look at him."

The triggerfish nosed closer to the platform, appearing ready to leap out of the water. To be closer to her, no doubt.

Lord knew Peter would probably act the same way. He couldn't wait to get her alone in his cabin, as it was. "Okay. Let me get something to carry him to the lab. I've got a samples aquarium he can stay in until we're back to shore." He looked at the fish. "That okay with you, Pentri?"

The fish turned sideways and eyed him, as if listening. Peter chuckled.

Behind him, Jack hollered, "Fishing trawler on the way. Probably coming to pull in that net." The captain slid down the ladder. "Talking to dolphins again?"

"Yeah," said Peter, meeting him well away from the platform's view. "Could I get you to take one more look at the engine? Maybe the fishermen have a patch we can buy."

"Sure. Where's that woman of yours?" Jack leered and touched the bill of his hat.

"What woman?" Peter carefully schooled his features.

Captain Serfass blinked then gave his head a brisk shake. "Uh… Hell, I dunno. Don't pay me any mind." He headed into the core of the boat, mumbling and scratching his neck.

With one obstacle out of the way, Peter ran to the lab and located a large blue bucket. On deck, he handed it to Ayprial, and she placed it in the water. Pentri swam in as if he didn't want to be anywhere else. Astounded, Peter lugged the triggerfish to the lab and put him in the aquarium. He grabbed the towel from his cabin and raced back to the platform.

"We've got to get you back inside. Right now. That is, unless you've changed your mind about staying." *Please stay.*

"I want to be with you."

His heart leapt at her words. Draping the towel over her tail, he scooped her into his arms and carried her to the cabin.

He shut the door with his foot, and after setting her on the bed, locked it. "Why don't you take that T-shirt off? It can't be comfortable sticking to you like that. And I don't want you getting a chill." Before she could move to do as he asked, however, he held up a finger and said, "Be right back."

In the lab, he picked up the satellite phone. Without the power booster, the call would probably have delays in transmission. He dialed his sister and waited for her to answer.

"Hello?"

"Hey, Erica. It's Peter." *Please be in a good mood.*

"Hey, there. I thought you were on the ocean today." She sounded cheerful, thank goodness.

"I am. I expect we'll be back at the research center's docks around eight o'clock this evening." If the trawler had a patch. If not, they'd have to call for a tow and might not make it back before morning. And he would do everything in his power to prevent spending the night on that boat with Jack. "I need a huge favor."

"Sure. What is it?"

This was too easy. "I need you to meet us when we get back. Bring some clothes."

"Why?"

Now, that was more like his sister. "Can't you just do me a favor without asking questions?" He smiled and waited for it.

"No."

He stifled a laugh. "I've got someone with me. She needs something to wear so she can leave the boat."

His sister released a delighted squeal. "A girl! Peter, it's about time. But why doesn't she have any clothes?"

"Her clothes got soaked," he lied. "She doesn't have a change. I just need you to bring her some." At the prospect of meeting a potential girlfriend, something Erica had ridden him about getting for three years, she'd be waiting at the docks when he returned.

"You called the right person. I'm always there for someone in need," she said.

He swallowed a laugh. "Eight o'clock. I'll call you if we can't make it by then."

"Sounds good. Talk to you later." She hung up.

Putting the phone away, he snapped his head toward the door at the sound of shouts above deck. The trawler had arrived. Popping his head in at his stateroom, he found Ayprial asleep. He closed the door and went to meet the fishermen. She needed her rest after everything she'd endured.

"...our scallop net," the trawler's captain was saying to Jack.

"Yeah. We hauled it up from the wreck. You're welcome to it. We just need to get our anchor out of it," said Captain Serfass.

Peter went to the side and shaded his eyes against the sun with his hand. "I had to cut it to retrieve a sample. Sorry about that."

The trawler captain waved a dismissive hand. "Don't much care about the net. It's the rigging I came back for. It's right expensive to replace. I appreciate your rescuing it for me."

"No problem," said Jack.

"Can I pay you for the salvage?"

Peter exchanged a look with Captain Serfass. "As a matter of fact, we've got a failed CAT engine," said Jack. "We need a valve patch to get us back to shore. You wouldn't, by any chance, have something we can use, do you?"

"Even exchange?"

"You bet," said Peter.

"I think we've got a patch that'll do you." The other captain picked up a walkie-talkie and spoke into it, and a minute later, a stocky man in dungarees arrived on the trawler's deck with a rolled section of sheet gasket tucked under an arm and carrying a pail of black greasy sealant.

Within an hour, Jack had the engine working, and the trawler pulled in the last of the scallop net's rigging and waved goodbye. Happier than ever before, Peter left the return voyage in Jack's capable hands and returned to the beauty sleeping in his cabin.

When he opened the door, Ayprial sat up and blinked at him. Her gorgeous eyes stole his breath. He closed and locked the door then turned in time to see her offer him a sweet, tentative smile. Unable to take his eyes off her, he could only stand and stare.

"Why do you...? I..." Speechless? That was a first.

"You're my lifemate, Peter." She held out a hand to him.

A wave of need washed over him. Not only need for her body, but need for her love, her approval, her respect. The intensity of it rocked him, and he took a staggering step forward. "Your lifemate?"

She nodded. "My forever. My love. The father of my children. I can be with no other. My heart is bound to yours."

He hadn't known how much he wanted to hear that until she spoke the words. He nearly collapsed under the weight of relief. As if dragged from his lips, he said, "You're my lifemate, Ayprial. My forever. My love. The mother of my children. I can be with no other. My heart is bound to yours."

He gasped, released from some kind of spell. Something major had happened. In a mystical, magical ceremony, they had committed to one another. The joining of their souls was as real as any physical joining, and a rush of love like nothing he'd ever experienced flooded him, expanding his heart, making her even more beautiful than before.

Closing the distance, he slid a hip to the mattress and wrapped her in his embrace. Her warmth and sweet fragrance surrounded him. "What just happened?" he whispered.

"We're mated for life. I'll be with you always. We'll never be alone again." She hugged him close and kissed the curve of his neck. "I love you."

In that moment, he needed to be inside her as surely as he needed air and water to live. As though reading his mind, she turned her face and captured his mouth with hers. He kissed her with a fierceness that spoke of his hunger. Ayprial was *the one*. No other woman could ever measure up to her. He knew it to his very core.

Breaking the kiss, he labored for breath and looked into her blue-green eyes. Where before he had only seen confusion and innocence, now he saw strength and intelligence. She was his match in every way. He smiled, and she returned it with a sexy, toothy grin.

Sending her fingers into his hair, she lay back and drew him on top. Her hot skin felt like silk under his questing palms. Taking a pebbled nipple between his lips, he drew on it until she moaned.

At his back, she bunched the fabric of his shirt and pulled it off of him. He removed his shorts and underwear while moving to her other breast to lavish it with his tongue's attention. Her fingers went back into his hair, and she let loose a raspy, two-toned groan that had him instantly hard. Tracing a fingertip down her lovely abdomen, he dipped it into her moist folds and found her wet and ready.

She opened for him. "Now, Peter. Please, now."

"Yes!" He kneeled between her trembling thighs and entered in a single thrust that made them both gasp. He shuddered, loving how she took all of him. A perfect fit.

She encircled his back with her legs, open and wanting. He stroked into her buttery passage and closed his eyes. Her soft whimpers of pleasure encouraged him to a faster pace, and she gripped his shoulders, meeting him thrust for thrust. Yes! Yes! Yes! Oh, God!

Her slick walls gripped his length, milking him and pulling him deeper. Her release sent him into his own, and he bucked in explosive orgasm. Ah-ah-ah! He clenched his jaw as the burning heat of pure ecstasy shot through him. Opening his eyes halfway, he watched her passion-filled expression, her mouth open on a silent scream, as she came with him. It took him to the edge and finished him. With one final thrust, he released his last into her. One with her. Belonging to her and not wanting to be anywhere else.

"Yes," he whispered. "I love you, too."

Spent, he withdrew and fell to the mattress. She rolled to her side, and he gathered her close, spooning her body to his. He buried his nose in her hair and inhaled. It smelled sweet, almost floral. Like her. Everything about her was sweet. Closing his eyes, he saw their future together. Like a movie, it played in his mind's eye. With her knowledge of ocean languages, her intelligence and excitement for learning, he would bring her into his work. Together, they would set the ocean science community on its ear. And their love for one another…Good Lord, so powerful. They faced a lifetime of joy.

Peter smiled and shook his head. He'd known her only hours, yet she completed him. He'd never felt such a part of someone the way he did with her. "No doubt."

"No doubt," she whispered.

Yes. No doubt whatsoever, they would live happily ever after.

The End

FOREVER
By Laura Kitchell

Caught in the rocks during a terrible storm, a mermaid gets rescued by an unlikely human – a novelist turned lighthouse keeper. Through the course of the night, he helps her heal and offers friendship; but what will come when the storm passes and the light of day offers her a chance to return to the sea? And can he let her go?

To Catch A Dream
(In the Merlicious Digest, or single)

Sargo, a mermaid princess, must convince Paul, a human, that he's a merman, a king, and he has to marry her.

You can email Laura at lkitchell@exis.net

FOREVER
By Laura Kitchell

Chapter One

Gavin finished his meager meal, which didn't agree with the knots in his stomach. He glared at a thin lighthouse manual someone had left him on the kitchen table. It appeared to be leftover from the nineteen-fifties. *Yeah, I'm way over my head here. What was I thinking?* The night promised to try his patience. He didn't look forward to it.

Around the curve of his lighthouse, wild wind created an ominous howl. *His* lighthouse. Good Lord. How hard a time would the county board give him if he asked them to release him from this job? He sighed and walked his dishes to the sink, the window above showing nothing in the deep, fathomless night.

Gavin's heart skipped a beat. The lighthouse beacon was out.

He dropped his plate and fork. They missed the basin and slid to the floor with a loud clatter. Not bothering with the mess, he grabbed the manual and raced for the stone staircase. He took steps two at a time, wishing he had less to climb. Every second counted when the lamp went out.

He snatched a heavy-duty flashlight from a hook at the top of the winding stairs then headed up a ladder to a hatchway. Gulping, Gavin pushed open the trapdoor. He didn't mind the height. He didn't mind the darkness, either. But the thought of entering a room made entirely of glass while lightning flashed, thunder boomed, and wind shook the wooden house below made him pause.

Closing his eyes, he braced a hand on the opening's edge. Visions flashed through his mind of shattering windows and driving rain. For a moment, his ears filled with screams and the deafening boom of thunder. He shook off the terrifying memory with some difficulty. He had work to do.

Releasing a long, slow breath, he climbed the three remaining steps. He flicked the flashlight's switch and willed his heart to slow its rapid tattoo. He could not afford this weakness. Lives on the popular shipping lane depended on him.

With renewed purpose, he ignored the eerie screech of gale-force winds whipping along the topmost ridge of the lighthouse's glass dome. He followed illustrated instructions in the manual to find the off switch on the ancient lamp's gas-powered pivot motor. He located a spare bulb in the adjacent cabinet. The last spare bulb. He swore under his breath.

"Temporary insanity. That's it. I temporarily lost my mind when I agreed to take this job in this stinkin' lighthouse."

The manual showed him how to switch out one of the burned bulbs for the last replacement, and a bright glow rewarded him for a job well done. Turning off his flashlight, he topped the fuel then nudged the pivot motor switch with his foot and waited a moment to make sure everything worked.

Shuddering, he went to the far wall of glass and gazed at the raging ocean. He refused to let the storm get the better of him. Rain blew in sideways sheets, battering the thick windows to no effect. At first, nothing beyond the rain and an occasional leaf held much interest. The light swung around, however, and shot through the darkness to reveal a merchant tanker laden with cargo and rocking on dangerous seas perilously close to craggy boulders on the shoreline.

Crewmembers sprinted along the ship's deck, and the light on the bridge blinked twice before a long, low horn sounded. Gavin waved, acknowledging the 'thank you.'

He let his gaze drop, contemplating an early night, but before he could turn in retreat, he caught a movement where crashing waves pounded the rocky shore. He squinted. Had he imagined it?

Then a pale, thin arm shot into the air. Delicate fingers grappled for an outcropping but missed and slid away.

Gavin's breath caught in his throat. Heaven help him, somebody had gone overboard.

* * * *

Draya cried out. She was trapped. Caught.

Her stomach sinking, she watched her sister helplessly follow the ship. Lindee had warned her not to accompany her to the surface, but Draya never passed an opportunity for adventure. Lindee's destiny waited on that cargo liner, and nothing Draya did or said could keep her sister from him.

Not that Draya would. She adored the romance and magic that brought mermaids to their life-mates. She understood the instinctual draw and inescapable bond that led her sister. She wanted the same. And despite the odd match, she would never question God's choice of a human for Lindee.

Grunting with the effort to free her tail from a fissure between two boulders at the shoreline, she desperately wished the magic that carried her sister after the ship were weaker so Lindee could help with this predicament before seeking her husband.

The strongest swimmer of all her sisters, Draya never let the sea overpower her. But a moment before the lighthouse's bright beam cut into the angry waves, she lost her rhythm. Lindee had screamed when Draya went careening to the boulders. She didn't want to imagine what her sister thought happened to her.

Draya's back burned with lacerations and her head felt ready to split open where it had hit. She moaned as she let her arm drop to her side. Her sister, now a pale movement barely discernable from the whitecaps of the turbulent sea, followed the ship as if connected by an invisible rope.

Clenching her teeth, Draya braced her arms against the immovable rock and tried to wrench her tail free. She pulled so hard a rip formed where the boulder's crags refused to release their hold in her scales. Crying out as the fire of pain raced to her brain, she began to despair.

A huge wave rose high then slammed into her. In the eddy of the wash, she fisted her hands as the forced pressure scraped her back and forth across the rough rocks, deepening her wounds and creating new ones. Gasping, she arched with searing pain. She closed her eyes and tried to calm her rising panic.

When she opened them, a bright yellow figure loomed over her. Draya screamed, sure a legendary land creature had come to steal her soul.

"It's okay! It's okay!" a man yelled above the roar of the stormy ocean.

He leaned close and she caught a flash of kind eyes as the lighthouse beam passed. The residual light reflected on a monstrous wave looming for a fresh pounding. He'd be knocked into the ocean. And with her tail wedged in the rocks, she couldn't help.

Before he could move away, she grabbed him around the middle and grasped her wrist to lock the hold. The wave crested and she braced.

"Hey! Let go. I'm trying to help you." The man resisted her hug.

Then the wave crashed. The water came onto them with a crushing weight, pressing the man against her. Draya held tightly despite protesting ribs.

When the water began to recede, the pull threatened to drag the man with it. He cried out, scrabbling for a handhold on the rocks.

"I have you," she said in his ear, not knowing how she sounded so calm. But it was true. Regardless of his slick raincoat, she had him under the arms, and as long as he didn't lift his hands, she could keep him atop her.

The last of the wave sluiced from the boulder. Pushing, the man got to his feet and wiped water from his lashes. He started to say something but a bolt of lightning struck the ocean with a noisy sizzling sound right before an enormous boom of thunder shook the earth. He stiffened and his eyes widened so much she expected him to scream. He didn't.

"Are you okay?" Draya asked after the thunder subsided.

"Yeah," he said, coming out of his daze. "We've got to get you out of here." He gave her a once over, really looking at her for the first time. "Where's your life jacket?"

"My what?" She wiggled, but her tail remained caught between the rocks.

His gaze drifted from her face, taking in her halter and naked midsection. "Someone on the ship's crew should've made you put on a life jacket."

"I wasn't on the ship."

He paused as his gaze reached her tail. His lips formed an O and his brows arched. "You're not from the ship, are you?"

"I just said I wasn't. Are you going to help me or not?"

The man gave his head a shake. "Yeah. Yeah. You're stuck?"

Draya nodded then regretted it as an inferno of pain tore through her brain. She gasped and shivered. When she found her voice, she said, "My tail is jammed in that fissure."

Raging wind sent the rain horizontal, the drops feeling more like pellets on her skin. Her entire body hurt.

The man didn't move. "I don't believe what my eyes are seeing."

"You better, and quickly. The storm is building."

As if to prove her right, another lightning strike zapped the ocean close enough to raise the hairs on her arms. Simultaneously, thunder cracked the heavens and threatened to deafen her.

The man yelled, his eyes wide in the flash. He went to his knees and placed violently shaking hands on her tail where it lodged against the boulder. Was he cold…or terrified? Pressing with his fingertips, he probed the point where she disappeared into the fissure.

"That hurts," Draya said, doing all she could to keep from crying out in pain.

"You're caught tight. And I can't really see."

The sky went to pitch and the rain thickened, making it impossible for her to see, too. Though he kneeled at her side, she found it difficult to discern his outline against the choppy ocean.

Another wave pounded the shore, stealing her breath and knocking the man across her hips. Neither had seen it coming. Draya grabbed the man's collar and held on, fearing he would slip to his death. He flung an arm over her tail and hugged, making her yell in agony as another rend formed along her scales. Her back raked against the rocks and she arched.

Immediately, a tidal wave surged, pushing her down. Like a hand on her forehead, the water shoved her head and everything went black.

•

Chapter Two

Gavin fought for air, his lungs on fire while the water receded. He couldn't believe he didn't get washed into the drink. What kind of crazy dream was he trapped in, anyway? One likely to get him killed if he didn't get the mermaid freed…or let her die.

Mermaid. The saltwater cleared and he sucked air into his lungs with a loud gasp. Mermaid. Had he lost his mind altogether? Or had he fallen asleep at his laptop and let the mermaid paintings in the house come to life in his dreams? If not, why wasn't he more freaked out by her?

He shook his head. It didn't matter. The storm reduced him to a quivering wreck with horrifying memories racing through his mind. He had to get this done before he lost the ability to function altogether. Trying to rise and failing, he realized she still had him by the hood of his raincoat.

"You can let go now." Rain beat against his features and stung his eyes. When she didn't release her hold, he took her hand and plucked it away so he could move.

Crawling along the rock, he struggled to maintain his balance on hands and knees until he could clearly see her face. Water ran in rivulets over her closed lids. She slept? No, impossible. Something had gone wrong.

He threw his weight to the fissure where her tail disappeared. Still lodged, she didn't budge as he tried to find a way to free her. The storm grew in intensity and Gavin began to think they would both perish. He couldn't let that happen. He refused to surrender, and he certainly wouldn't abandon this stranded creature.

Shoving his hands into the crag, he jammed his fingers as far between her rough, muscular tail and the abrasive rock as he could manage. He pulled with all his might, yelling with effort as the skin on his knuckles threatened to flay. Her tail loosened, but at the expense of further injury.

A triple flash of lightning showed a tremendous swell of ocean headed their way. A tremor shot through him, paralyzing him for a moment. Though not a wave, the dark water would overtake him. He fought past his fear and the urge to run. He had to try harder. He wouldn't fail. Not this time.

He made another attempt to pull her free, but she bled. Her blood mixing with salt water created a slippery film over the scales of her tail. Digging in his fingertips, he clenched his jaw and pulled.

She began to slide free, but his hands were losing their grip. He couldn't maintain the pressure.

The ocean swell arrived, but instead of flooding over the boulder, it met the rock-face head-on. Momentum behind the swell forced water through the crack in a great blast. It shot straight up like a geyser and pushed her tail.

Free! She was free. Gavin leaned into a gust of wind and grabbed the mermaid around the waist. Thankful for the lamp's glow as it swung around and lit his way, he used all his strength to sling her over his shoulder and scramble off the rocky shoreline before another wave could knock them into the sea.

On shaky legs, he ran across slick grass that fronted the lighthouse, grunting under her weight. As thin as she appeared, he guessed she must weigh close to two hundred pounds. All tail. All muscle. His feet slipped and slid the entire way.

He flung open the door and it bounced against his luggage still waiting in the entrance. "Not exactly how I imagined my first night," he grumbled.

As he carried the mermaid to the back of the house, the phone began to ring. The high-pitched bell on the old-fashioned telephone grated on his nerves, despite his attempt to ignore it. In the bedroom next to his, he laid her on the bed then hurried to the kitchen.

"Hello?" he said, picking up the handset on the fifth ring. He despised the tremble in his voice. *Man up, Billings. It's just a storm.*

"Mr. Billings? I wanted to call and make sure you have everything under control."

Gavin fought the urge to snap at the town's mayor. "Mayor Langston, I don't know what kind of maintenance program you had for this lighthouse before you hired me, but all the bulbs were out. A tanker almost crashed on the rocks before I had a chance to replace one. Replace one, I'll add, with the *only* good bulb in the place."

The man spluttered. "I-I-I…well, Mr. Billings, what can I say? The old lighthouse keeper took care of all those particulars. When he passed away last year, the town's board was in transition, what with the elections and all. The subject never came up…"

Gavin couldn't abide the excuses. "The house is in disrepair, the lighthouse machinery needs servicing, and the grounds need work. As I understand it, the state provides funds for the lighthouse's upkeep. I want all they've paid since the old keeper passed away. I'll order an accounting if I have to."

"That won't be necessary, Mr. Billings. I'll have my secretary take care of it tomorrow. I'm just grateful to you for taking this position on such short notice. Our citizens were ready to riot over the idea of losing control of the lighthouse. We take great pride—"

"Mayor Langston, I'm really busy. I haven't even unpacked."

"Of course. I'll let you go then. Call me if you need anything. With this nor'easter blowing through, I imagine you'll be up all night watching over the shoreline."

Gavin sighed. The night had already seemed endless, yet it was still early. "I have your number."

"Goodnight."

Kiss my ass. He replaced the telephone's handset and shook his head. *That man's useless.* Stripping off his wet raincoat, he dropped it to the kitchen floor and left his sopping boots and socks next to it. His other clothes clung to him, wet too, but he couldn't get naked with a mermaid in the house.

A mermaid. He slapped a palm to his forehead. When would this nightmare end? Rushing to the room where he'd left her, he hoped to find it empty. Maybe he'd imagined the whole thing. The soaking pants clinging to his legs refused to let him hope.

Sure enough, her form still monopolized the bedspread. He had a sick mermaid in his house and no idea how to help her. As he contemplated whether he should change into dry clothes or examine her wounds first, it occurred to him that something had changed. He couldn't make out much more than her shadow on the bed in the dark of the room, so he flicked on the light.

The world came to a screeching halt. She still wore her halter-top but her tail was gone. In its place curled two shapely, battered legs that led to gently flaring hips. His body responded instantly, his mouth going dry as his blood burned like molten lava through his veins.

Embarrassed, he ducked out and hurried into his own bedroom. He had no time for this. A storm raged, tearing at the shingles on the roof and making the windows rattle in their panes. He had to somehow ensure that the one working bulb in the lighthouse beacon burned through the night. And he had an injured, unconscious, practically bare mermaid—no, not mermaid—woman in his guest room. She needed his help, not his horniness.

He couldn't help her until he got some control, though. With a huff, he gathered supplies from the medicine cabinet in his less-than-master master bathroom, wondering only briefly how long they'd been in there, and padded to her room.

She had flipped to her stomach and now stirred. Gavin grimaced at the sight of her gashed back. Black and purple bruising marred her porcelain color in too many places between shoulders and ankles. Still, it surprised him how little she bled. Considering the abuse she'd taken and the tearing he'd witnessed, she had scabbed quickly and oozed only in a few places.

"Why are you just standing there?" she asked. "Are you afraid of me?"

"No." Okay, maybe a bit. He averted his gaze and found himself staring at a cheesy mermaid painting hanging crooked on the wall. First thing tomorrow, it would go in the trash.

"Then come in." She winced, her features pinching with pain.

He couldn't. Not with her lying practically naked like that. "I'll be right back." He dumped the medical supplies on a small table inside the doorway and retreated.

"Hey!" she yelled.

Ignoring her, he searched for a closet. He discovered one near the end of the short hallway and breathed a sigh of relief at stacks of clean sheets and towels. Snatching a sheet off the top, he marched to her room. He didn't hesitate to go in this time, though he gulped and tried not to stare at her way too shapely, way too long legs.

With one hand, he shook the sheet until it came unfolded. It was a fitted sheet. What the hell? Who folded fitted sheets square? Well, he had no intention of leaving again. He might be tempted not to return, and she needed help.

He draped the elastic-edged linen over her, grateful it covered her from shoulder to knees. "So what's your name?"

"Draya," she answered through clenched teeth.

"I'm Gavin Billings. Nice to meet you." *I think.*

She passed him a skeptical grimace. "Are you serious? Please tell me you have some pain reliever. Tylenol? Advil? Something."

He arched a brow. "So you know about our ways?"

"Your *ways*?" She laughed despite her pain. "I live right off the coast. I'm no stranger."

He chuckled. "Sorry." He dragged the small table with his supplies from the wall to the bedside and singled out a bottle of generic pain reliever. He measured a dose into his palm and hazarded a glance at her face. She was stunning, with fine features like a nymph, plump lips the color of red plums, and turquoise eyes that seemed to glow blue from between a set of long, jet black lashes curling to arched brows. He gulped and felt her forehead. He didn't like the heat coming off of her, but the pain reliever would reduce a fever…if she actually had one. "What's your normal temperature?"

"I don't know. I've never had to take it before. May I have some water to take these with?"

Right. Water. He hurried to the kitchen.

"Put some salt in it for me," she called then groaned.

Salt. Ocean. Right. He sprinkled salt from a shaker into a glass of tap water and rushed to her.

She accepted the glass and downed the pills. "Ugh. Not enough salt."

He took the water and set it on the table. Easing the sheet upward to reveal the gashes on her thigh, he asked, "So how did you wind up on those rocks?"

"I'm not sure. It happened so fast. It must have been a wave." She frowned and whispered, "It *must* have been."

Dabbing with a peroxide-soaked cotton ball, he let foam dotted with tiny pebbles and dirt rise from the wound before clearing it away with a washcloth. "Is it normal for you to be out and about in the midst of storms like this?"

As if to underscore his question, a clap of thunder shook the house and made his heart skip a beat. He shivered and pulled at the wet T-shirt clinging to his chest.

"Out and about?"

Gavin swallowed against a familiar discomfort. "I'm not gay. I'm a writer."

"What kind of writer?" She rolled her eyes toward the wall above the headboard while biting her bottom lip.

"I'm sorry." He hated that he had to hurt her in order to help her. "I'll be done in a minute. I promise. I write novels. Well…one novel so far." Satisfied the wounds looked clean enough, he squeezed antibacterial ointment along the length of the deepest abrasion then covered it with a soft gauze bandage. "Other side."

"Other side? What does that mean?" she asked, the graceful arches of her brows coming together in a frown.

"It means I need to tend the injury on your other side."

"Oh." She sounded weak.

He had to get her mind off his ministrations. As she rolled, he searched for a topic that would get her talking. He settled on one in perfect time. "You didn't answer my question."

"I did," she argued. "I'm not sure how I got caught in the rocks."

He smiled, glad for the strength seeping into her spirited tone. "I mean the one about you being out in the storm. I can't think why anyone would want to be out in that mess."

"That's right. I got sidetracked with that whole 'out and about' business."

"Are you teasing me?"

She didn't answer.

He scowled at the back of her head. A part in her damp curls revealed a knot with an angry cut. Gavin looked from her head to her leg and determined the head wound needed attention first. "This is going to hurt." He pressed a gauze pad to the large bump.

She gasped and shuddered. "You wouldn't believe me if I told you," Draya said with a voice tight with pain.

"I just rescued a creature of myth from some nasty rocks amidst a raging nor'easter. I can't believe I went out there. I don't handle storms. At all. And now I'm tending your injuries. At this point, I'd believe just about anything."

Chapter Three

Draya awoke stiff. It felt like the lightning flashing outside cut right through her brain instead. Clutching the back of her head, her hand met with a soft bandage that wrapped around and covered her brow.

Rocks. Lindee. Gavin. Terrible pain. She groaned.

Rolling, she took in the quaint room lit by nearly constant flashes. Thunder rumbled unending, interrupted by occasional claps that shook her bed. A wail wavered through the ceiling. Was that a man's shout?

Where was that kind man? He'd said something about storms. *I can't believe I went out there. I don't handle storms. At all.*

Lightning exploded outside her window and she jerked upright with a shriek. Her head throbbed, and for a moment, she thought she might pass out. In the lull between the lightning strike and the thunder, she distinctly discerned a man's shout.

Draya staggered from the bed. Had Gavin gotten hit by lightning? Did he need her help? Her legs and back no longer hurt, healing fast thanks to her mermaid immune system, but her head protested every move she made. Pulling the bandage off her head, she dropped the gauze to the floor. She tied the elastic-edged sheet around her hips and shuffled from the room.

The entire house stood in darkness, but the bright storm lit her way toward the door with intermittent bursts of light. Another shout sounded outside the door, then it flew open and hit the wall with a bang.

With her stomach at her feet, Draya took a startled step backward. A flash backlit a broad shouldered figure who swaggered in.

"Hey there," Gavin rasped, breathless and dripping. A bolt of light revealed his haggard features as he closed the door and removed his boots. In one hand, he gripped a hammer, and he clutched a wide board under his arm. "Did I frighten you?"

"A little," she admitted. "I thought you hate storms." Why hadn't she noticed before what a sexy shape he had? Those shoulders, that chest and his ridged and narrow waist showing clearly under a T-shirt plastered to him by the rain would give any merman competition for a mermaid's affection. Where was the yellow coat he'd worn when he rescued her?

He offered her an attempted smile that came across more like a grimace. "I do. Can't stand them. But if I absolutely have to go out in one, yelling helps."

She couldn't decide whether to be appalled or amused. "You didn't scream when you were helping me."

"Okay, I don't *scream*. I yell. And I was yelling. In my mind." He tapped a finger to his temple, his bicep flexing, and set the board and hammer on an end table.

"You're soaking."

He looked miserable. "Yeah. That tends to happen in the rain. What're you doing out of bed?"

"I heard you shout. I was coming to help." She realized now she would hinder more than help. Agonizing stabbing pain made her eyes cross, and the world tipped.

"Whoa!" In an instant, Gavin reached her and swept her into his arms. He used so much strength he actually tossed her slightly before catching her. "You're much lighter without your tail."

She was?

"Am I hurting you?"

Draya squeezed her eyes closed, loving the feel of his hands on her and overwhelmed with the desire to kiss him. "No."

He carried her to the bedroom and nudged her discarded bandage with his toe. To his credit, he didn't say anything, though he arched his brows and gave her a critical look. He set her on the bed. She sat, though, reluctant to release her hold around his neck. She couldn't stand this weakness, and he offered a steady strength she found irresistible.

"You should sleep," he advised.

"I'm not tired. What were you doing outside?" *Please talk to me so I don't sit here worrying about Lindee out there in this storm.*

"Let me see if I can get the power on. I'll be right back."

She drew her knees to her chest and hugged her arms around them. The storm blustered, making it impossible for her to ignore it. Blinding flashes hurt her eyes, so she closed her lids and rested her cheek against a knee. When the pain between her eyes didn't dissipate, she figured her head injury caused it.

After a few minutes, a golden glow intruded on the darkness behind her lids. She opened her eyes to light spilling from a lamp in the living room. Moving slowly, she scooted from the bed and went to the doorway. She flipped a switch that turned on an overhead globe at the center of the bedroom ceiling. Somehow, it took the edge off the flashes. Even the thunder sounded less threatening.

Gavin came around a corner with a towel around his neck. "Much better. Hey, what're you doing up?" He offered a crooked smile. "You're stubborn, aren't you?"

She smiled. "My father would agree, and add a few other words to describe me."

"Such as?"

She felt for the footboard and settled backward onto the edge of the mattress. "Obstinate. Reckless. Disrespectful."

He came to the doorway and leaned against the frame. "I would guess more like headstrong, adventurous, and independent."

"You might have it right."

The look in his eyes, a mixture of humor and admiration, caused her stomach to flutter. She appreciated the intelligence shining in his gaze. A boom of thunder rattled the room's sole window and made the entire house tremble.

Gavin's knees gave and he took a lunging step for the bed. "I'll just sit here next to you."

Draya bit her lip. He clearly suffered, and she didn't want to laugh. "Now tell me why you had a hammer and board out there."

"Leaking roof." He ruffled the towel over his hair then wiped it over his face.

"It couldn't wait?"

"This nor'easter could blow all night. With rain pouring in, the living room would've been a pool by morning. I already dread seeing what condition the floorboards are in under that ratty carpet. Adding a flood would only make it worse."

She wanted to lie down but he blocked her way, so she leaned against him. His firm body accepted her weight. It lent her courage. "If it's so bad, why do you live here?"

"Actually, I don't. I mean, I didn't." He sighed and wrapped his arms around her.

She relaxed, finding on unexpected comfort in his embrace. Placing her cheek against the end of the towel that hung over one shoulder and part of his chest, she fingered droplets of rain clinging to dark hairs on his arm.

He cleared his throat. "I took the job from an internet job finder site and just got here today. I haven't even unpacked."

"You accepted a job without seeing the place first? Wasn't that risky?" He impressed her more and more by the minute.

"Yeah. And not smart, apparently. But Barnes County was desperate for a lighthouse keeper and I was desperate to get away."

"Why?"

"Long story."

"Good. It'll pass the time." She snuggled closer and brought her feet onto the bed.

"Well, it's not really a long story. I guess it won't hurt to tell you. I'd lost my job—a boring one as an oil change mechanic for a trucking company in a small town in Nebraska. I had some money saved and dreamt of writing a novel, so I figured there'd never be a better time. It was harder than I thought, and by the time I finished the story, I'd run out of money. I couldn't believe it when I sold the book right away. I didn't think I could do it again, so I spent my advance on bills and went looking for a job. But it was too late."

"Too late to find a job? I don't understand." Draya shifted to get a look at his face.

His features twisted into an uncomfortable mask of embarrassment. "You see, I'd used people from around town as characters in my book, and I changed names, but not much. The book turned out to be a best seller, hit the New York Times bestseller list in its second week, and well, the people in town started reading the thing."

"They weren't proud to have a famous author in their community?"

Draya snuggled against him, enjoying the feel of him way too much.

"Uh, no. In fact, there were some who were downright pissed with the way I'd portrayed them in my book. Namely, my landlord, who promptly evicted me, my ex-boss who told everyone I was a lazy worker so nobody would hire me, and the bank manager who *accidentally* emptied my account long enough for all my checks to bounce before correcting the balance. No, staying wasn't an option."

"Didn't you think when you were writing the story that those people would mind?"

He chuckled. "I didn't think I did all that great a job describing them, to be honest. I didn't think the book would ever get published, much less hit the bestseller list, and I definitely didn't think anyone would recognize those people. Man, was I wrong."

"So what made you take a job in a lighthouse so far from Nebraska?"

"You know, I'm not sure. I grew up down the street from a lighthouse and hung out with the old guy who kept it. He taught me a lot, but that was a long time ago."

"A lighthouse in Nebraska?"

He laughed, the movement jostling her in a wonderful way. "No. I grew up in North Carolina. Anyway, I saw the ad and was compelled to take the position. I figured it would be a quiet job with nobody breathing down my neck, and I could work on my next book."

"Then you got here…"

"And all hell broke loose."

"I'm sorry I caused you so much trouble." Maybe her father had it right when he said she should accept life and stop searching for thrills.

"This may sound strange, but you've been the best part of this whole experience."

Chapter Four

Gavin had more bravery than he'd given himself credit. But Draya brought it out in him. If not for her injuries and need of his care, he'd probably cower and whimper in his bedroom until the storm passed.

Then again, he *had* ventured into the top of the lighthouse and changed that bulb despite the thunder, lightning, and all the windows. Maybe he was meant to come to this place, after all. There seemed to be some kind of healing energy.

He rubbed a hand up and down her arm, mesmerized for a moment by how soft her skin felt. For a creature that lived in the ocean, she sure didn't feel like a fish…or smell like one. He discreetly dipped his nose into her fragrant curls and inhaled. Lilac? And maybe bergamot? Whatever it was, he liked the clean, sweet scent.

"Do you want to sleep?" he asked.

"No." She shivered.

"My wet clothes are making you cold. I'll go change." He moved to rise but she hugged an arm around him.

"Don't go."

"I'll just be a minute."

She hugged him tighter. "Please."

Did he detect fear in her plea? Fear he understood. He wouldn't leave her. "Okay. I'm here," he soothed. "It's alright."

Wind whipped around the corner of the house, shaking the wall behind the bed and causing the window to rattle. Another thunder boomer rocked the night. Closing his eyes, Gavin braced for the worst. He focused so hard, he barely noticed as Draya shifted.

Then his cold, wet shirt climbed the flexed muscles of his abdomen, followed by soft, warm hands that explored. He glanced down. She gazed at him with turquoise eyes practically glowing with desire. Breathtaking.

She pushed the sopping fabric higher until it bunched at his armpits. Off. Right, she wanted it off. He did, too. With one hand, he grasped the shirt and yanked it over his head. He tossed it through the doorway, and it landed on the vinyl tiles in the hall with a slap.

"These should come off," she said, slipping her fingertips under the band of his jeans.

"I don't know if that's a good idea." Except he wanted nothing more than to get out of his pants. He could practically smell her excitement and his body reacted.

"You're getting my bed wet." She grinned.

Sounded perfectly reasonable to him. "Of course. We can't have that." Gavin slid out from behind her and worked at removing his jeans. The stiff, damp cotton clung to his legs, making it difficult to manage. "Just give me a second," he said, his voice strained with effort as his clumsy hands shoved the pants past his knees.

He doubled over, pushing his jeans over his calves and trying not to yank out leg hair in the process. When he finally stepped from them, he slid his socks off too and tossed it all into the hall with his shirt. He wondered if she would ask him to take off his underwear. He hoped so.

He turned and went still. Draya stretched on her side atop the bedding, her halter-top and the sheet on the floor. Her lids drooped, giving her a sleepy, seductive look while she ran the tip of her tongue over her full and inviting bottom lip.

Slender shoulders and delicate collarbones contradicted the size of her high, plump breasts. With rose-colored nipples hardened and begging for his kisses, he couldn't help thinking human women paid good money for a world-class rack like that. He licked lips gone dry.

Her body dipped on a tiny waist then flared to hips that gave her a shape only one word could describe - voluptuous.

Long, sexy legs hiding her Venus mound bent slightly at the knees and tapered to narrow, dainty feet. His gaze found the bandage on her outer thigh and focused on the telltale red blotch staining the center of the gauze.

"We shouldn't." It actually *hurt* to say that. Gavin grimaced.

Draya followed his stare. "No, it's fine." She peeled the bandage from her leg. "See?"

He blinked and leaned closer, not believing his eyes. The raw gash that had worried him earlier now appeared hardly more than an angry scrape. "Good Lord. How in the—"

"I have a metabolized immune system. It keeps me from becoming shark bait when I get injured. Now take those off and come comfort me."

Oh, yeah. She wanted the underwear off as badly as he did. Surprised but glad about her wounds, he stripped bare. Already, his shaft pointed in her direction, making it clear to them both exactly what it wanted.

Thunder rumbled, sounding distant. He couldn't tell if the storm moved away or the pounding in his ears merely dampened the sound. "Are you sure about this?" They *were* practically strangers.

"I've never been more sure of anything." Opening her arms, she beckoned.

He'd never wanted anything more, either. He had a sense that if he tried to walk away now, he wouldn't make it to the doorway. Blood raced through his veins. He felt hot and alive. "What about your head?"

She touched fingers to the back of her hair as if she'd forgotten about it. "It's fine. Just don't bang it against the headboard." She grinned.

Gavin laughed and placed a knee on the bed next to her hip. "You're so beautiful."

"You are, too." Sitting, she met him for a kiss. As she pressed her lips to his, she sent a hand to the nape of his neck and drew him down.

He braced a hand next to her shoulder and combed fingers into her dark, silken curls. Everywhere their bodies touched, he caught fire. Her soft, warm skin enraptured him, making him want to wrap her around him. Deepening the kiss, he added pressure to her bottom lip and urged her to open.

She did. Her tongue touched the tip of his with a hesitant, curious test. Smiling against her mouth, he sent his tongue inside, drinking in the taste of her. She might eat fish, but she tasted like strawberries and vanilla. Hungry for more, he settled next to her and pulled her against him as he leisurely explored straight teeth, full lips, and agile tongue.

Her firm breasts pushed against his chest, her hard nipples teasing him. Unable to ignore them, he groaned his reluctance to break the kiss then worked his way along her arched throat to her collarbone. Pecking tender kisses along the length to her shoulder, he grasped her tight waist and slid lower.

She gasped as he took a nipple between his lips and gently sucked. Letting his hand skim upward to cup the side of her breast, he marveled at her satin texture. Everything about her tempted him, invited him to dive into her and lose himself.

"You're a siren," he said, moving to the other breast.

"No, you're the one weaving the spell," she said, her voice breaking on the last word as he gently clamped teeth on her nipple.

Draya lifted a knee, her leg caressing his as she moved her thigh to rest on his hip. He released her breast and shifted upward to capture her eager mouth. Reaching between them, she grasped his steely length. He ached to be inside her but didn't want to rush. She felt so good, smelled so sweet, he wanted to savor every moment. Tomorrow, she would likely return to the sea, and he had only one night to get his fill of her.

Lightning flashed and thunder made the house tremble on its foundation. It didn't frighten him. Instead, the deep rumble that followed echoed the thrumming need coursing through him. The storm took on a different meaning. For the first time, it didn't carry a threat. His mind didn't instantly go to his living nightmare with every crash in the clouds. Just the opposite. Every flash and every boom celebrated the remarkable emotion, hunger, need and urgency that blossomed between them.

Draya ran smooth fingers over his shaft and he moaned, adoring her touch. Wanting to return the favor and test her readiness, he sent a finger into her cleft. She threw back her head and cried out her pleasure. Already, slick moisture awaited him. It coated his finger as he stroked her folds.

Hips undulating to match his movement, she clutched his shoulders and tensed. She lifted her head and gave him such an earnest look it stole his breath. A searing electric charge ripped through him, making him harder—something he didn't think possible.

He couldn't wait. She had done something to him, and he needed to sink into her heat. Now.

* * * *

She would go mad if Gavin didn't join with her. She'd indulged in flings with human men before, but this was different, more powerful. For some reason, Draya couldn't stand the idea of separating from him for even a minute. And if he didn't climb on top of her and connect their bodies, she'd come out of her skin.

She dropped her calf to his lower back and squeezed, needing him as she'd never needed anything in her life. "Now. Please."

Removing his finger from her throbbing crease, he rolled her onto her back and inserted a knee between her thighs. Then he hesitated. "We need protection."

"No!" *What's wrong with me?*

"I have some right—" He tried to back off the bed but stopped. The skin across his cheekbones pulled tight and his lips thinned as though he suffered. Coming near and settling between her legs, he panted. "I can't."

She understood. She'd felt it, too—an electric shock that struck her between the eyes when he'd moved to leave. Deep in her womb, a coil wound taut and promised to tear her in half if he didn't relieve the pressure.

"Gavin," she cried. "Please."

"What's happening?" he asked, his voice strained as he fitted the tip of his shaft to her opening.

"I don't know, but it's going to hurt if we don't do this." She wrapped her ankles behind his thighs and hooked her fingers over his shoulders. "Now. We can't wait."

"Aaah!" He drove into her, filling her on a single thrust.

"Yes!" they yelled at the same time.

It was both beautiful and terrifying. He came over her and placed his lips to hers in a slow, meaningful kiss. Though they'd come together in this joining as if outside of their control, he took the lead now and mastered the situation.

Draya sighed. The urgency had fled. Bit by bit, Gavin eased out to his tip then filled her. He repeated the move, setting a leisurely pace. The coil released its pressure. Relaxing, she explored him with her fingertips, learning his shape, his textures.

She repeated caresses or grazed nails along his skin as she learned by his telltale breathing where he liked to be touched. The dip where neck met shoulder, the curve of arm leading to his armpit, the bulge of muscle running the length of his ribs. Even the scruff of new beard growth at his jaw line. He fascinated her. She'd never enjoyed a man so much.

He released her mouth, and with a mischievous grin, rolled them, still connected, until she straddled him. She laughed, gazing onto his handsome features and running her fingers through the light dusting of hair on his chest then over the ridges of his stomach.

Their eyes met and the laughter died on her lips. But not the joy blooming inside her. The intense emotion shining from his gold-flecked green eyes matched the surge of affection softening her heart.

Rocking her hips, she massaged her walls around his length. With each undulation, her passage tightened and the coil that had tortured her before their joining returned with a spiraling need growing deep in her womb. His parted lips and hooded eyes reflected the pleasure she experienced. She sank her teeth into her lower lip. The hard resistance of his shaft produced a delicious friction.

"You feel so good," she said.

His expression grew more serious. Cupping her breasts, he skimmed the pads of his thumbs over her puckered nipples. The coil contracted another notch and she gasped. His palms rode her curves to her hips where he grasped her and helped set the rhythm.

It wasn't enough. The urgency returned. She needed him hard and fast. Flipping her to her back, Gavin took the lead once more. He took her lips in a passionate kiss while setting a pounding pace.

Draya clung to him, arms and legs secured around him as she met his every thrust. His eyes locked with hers and they became one. Connected. Inseparable. Her heart skipped a beat right before he swept her away on a climbing wave of pleasure.

The coil tightened, becoming unbearable as she strained for the crest. He cried out, his face a mask of pained concentration. Bracing above her on outstretched arms, he drove into her.

She stopped breathing, riding the peak with him until he pushed her into crashing ecstasy. She screamed, tumbling weightless and helpless in the rolling undertow of her orgasm. As if from a distance, she recognized Gavin's shout – a shout of release, followed by a tremendous blast of thunder.

He stopped moving within her, and she surfaced with a huge intake of air. Immediately, tears smarted. He had shaken her world, touched her soul, become part of her.

"My God," he whispered, breathing as if he'd just finished swimming a race. He settled to the bed beside her. "Was that thunder or my brain exploding?"

She laughed and blinked against the wetness perched on her lower lids. "I couldn't tell. My own brain was exploding."

"Please tell me I'm not alone in thinking we just shared an amazing event. Is it like this every time for mermaids?"

"Wow. No, you're not alone." She snuggled closer and rested her cheek on his shoulder. "Something monumental happened between us tonight. And no, it's never been like this for me with anyone but you."

Draya pressed her nose to his skin, liking his scent—an interesting and intoxicating combination of ocean, soap, and something rich and spicy all his own. She kissed the side of his neck and ran fingertips through crisp hairs sprouting from the dip at the center of his chest. A swirl of finer, smooth hair hugged the stretch of muscle above his nipples, and she ran her palm over them.

"Mmm. I'll give you an hour to stop that," he said, closing his eyes. His hand played at the curve of her waist above her hip. "You're the sexiest woman I've ever met."

A stab of sadness cut deep into her stomach. "I'm not a woman," she said quietly. "I'm a mermaid."

He opened his eyes and stared. "You're going to leave."

She lowered her gaze, unable to face his disappointment. "I don't think I have a choice. I came to the surface with my sister, but I wasn't supposed to. She had her calling, and I came along for the fun of it. Then I got caught in the rocks. My father will worry if I don't return."

"Return to what?"

She despised the hurt in his voice that so perfectly mirrored the ache in her heart. Return to what, indeed?

Chapter Five

He wouldn't pressure her. She had to want to stay, to be with him of her own free will. Gavin wouldn't have her at his side any other way. But her silence was discouraging.

"I'd return to my life, which I wish was different," she said.

"Different how?"

"I see my friends called to meet their life-mates, and I wait. All my sisters but one have been called, including my younger sister, Lindee. She was called tonight. And what's for me?" She didn't use a complaining tone, but he detected loneliness in her words.

"Is that what you want? To be called to a life-mate?" The thought of her meeting another man, even a merman, made him clench his jaw in anger. What they'd shared was theirs—his and hers alone. He couldn't stomach the idea of her with anyone else.

Draya draped a possessive arm over his middle. "What I want is this. I've been missing this feeling. Wanting this connection."

"And what if you aren't called? Your sister who hasn't been called, for example. What if she's never called?"

"Once she goes in heat, Brandine will have to mate and bond…or die."

"Die?" That alarmed him like nothing else. "If you don't bond, you'll die?"

She held her silence a long moment. "I don't want to go. I'd rather stay and explore this thing we've discovered."

Gavin placed a kiss on her forehead. She felt much cooler. "Then stay here with me." *And don't die. Bond with me.*

She sighed heavily. "Is it okay if I change the subject?"

"Sure." *Rip out my heart.*

"Why do you shout in the storm?"

Not a subject he'd choose, but he found it strange how her asking didn't bother him. He'd never liked talking about it, but with her, his mind seemed more open. "It's something that happened when I was fifteen."

"A storm?"

"Yeah, as bad as this one."

As if to reinforce his statement, thunder rumbled then hail pelted the roof.

"Do you think the roof can handle this?" she asked.

"I hope so." He listened for breaches, but the house withstood the beating.

"Tell me more about why you shout."

"Well, it gets me through. Kind of takes my mind off the memories. You see, my family had moved to Nebraska to a town divided by a river. That storm caused the river to flood its banks. My sister was driving me home after basketball practice when the water came. It carried us right off the road and slammed us into the concrete wall of a mill. We hit so hard all the windows imploded. Glass went everywhere."

"That's awful," she said, hugging him close.

"I still have scars from the cuts." He showed her a few pale crescents on his arm. "That was just the beginning. My sister hit her head on the steering wheel and I couldn't rouse her. Before I could get us both out of our seatbelts, the water started pouring in. That car filled so fast." Gavin paused, expecting the usual wrenching agony that accompanied the memory. It didn't happen. Taking a deep, cleansing breath, he continued. "Her seatbelt jammed, so I backed out of my window. The water was nearly to the roof by then, and I had to hold onto the window frame to keep from getting swept away."

"You must have been so scared. You were just a boy."

"I was sure we'd both drown."

"Did you get her out?" She rose to an elbow and gazed at him with large, worried eyes.

So beautiful. He was consumed by *her* rather than the memory. Release from shame proved liberating. "Yes. I grabbed the collar of her shirt and pulled her out from under the seatbelt. It wasn't easy. Her lap strap held her to the seat, but I got it loose enough to get her out."

"And you were both okay?"

He shook his head. "The river was racing at that point, and the textile mill was smack in the middle. You can't imagine how fast that water was rushing around those walls. The second I let go of the car, it got struck by lightning. We both got burned. Then the water bashed us against the concrete. If I could have, I would have taken the hit to protect my sister. The water was crazy, though. She smashed head-first into the mill wall before we cleared the corner. The force of the current slammed us into the front wall, but I took that one with my shoulder. I still don't know how I managed to hold onto her." Where was the guilt? The shame?

"You were lucky to survive," she said, her lower lip trembling slightly.

All the times his sister had thanked him for saving her life finally sank in. "You're right. My sister has been paralyzed and in a wheelchair ever since, but she lived." *She lived.* For the first time, he realized how huge that was. "And I'm an idiot."

"Why do you say that?"

"Because I've spent these years blaming the storm for what happened, and blaming myself for my sister's paralysis. But you know what? There's no fault. My sister tried to make me see that it's not what life delivers that matters but what we do with it. She was so right, and I've been so blind. And stupid."

Thunder cracked into the night with the might of a bomb. He didn't have the urge to yell. He wasn't bombarded with images of breaking glass or surging water. Instead, he wanted to laugh. The nightmare was over. He was free.

"You saved her. You saved *me*." Draya cupped his jaw and stared into his eyes. "You're a hero. My hero." Leaning against him, her lush breasts pressing into his side, she lowered her lips to his.

* * * *

"Grant me a wish."

Draya laughed as Gavin rolled her onto her back. He cradled an arm under her neck, keeping her head off the bed, and she admired his care for her injury. "I'm not a genie."

"Conjure a spell." He grinned.

"I'm not a witch. You don't know much about mermaids, do you?"

He shrugged. "I haven't been on the coast since I was a kid. What do you expect?"

"You knew about sirens enough to accuse me of being one." Poking him playfully in the chest, she pecked a quick kiss on the curve of his unshaven chin.

He licked his lips and stared at her mouth. "Then tell me what mermaids do. I'm ignorant. Educate me."

"Kiss me first."

Her stomach quivered with delight as he lowered and fitted his lips to hers. She loved how his firm lips worked over hers, how his broad shoulders and muscled arms made her more delicate and feminine in comparison. Sending her fingers into his thick waves, she urged him deeper into the kiss and opened for him. Their tongues met and moisture wet her between the legs. It surprised her how just his kiss excited her so much.

With wind whipping around the edge of the house and making a squealing howl, he lifted out of the kiss. "How was that?"

"Heavenly." She hummed and trailed fingers along his neck. "Your hair is dry."

"Mmm. It's all this heat." He dipped his face to her throat where he placed soft kisses. "So tell me what mermaids do."

"Haven't you heard? We sit around on rocks and comb our hair." Draya bit her lip to keep from laughing.

Gavin stopped his efforts, making her mewl in disappointment. "No, really," he said. "I want to know."

"For your next book?"

"Maybe." He smirked.

"Well, we do a lot. We gather and garden. We tend phytoplankton blooms. We sing the whales to migration."

"Phytoplankton blooms?" He sat and found his towel.

She rose to her elbows. "Yes. Phytoplanktons are tiny plants that support all life in the ocean. When the waters warm and become clearer, they multiply. We help send them closer to the surface where the water is even warmer and sunlight can reach them. It makes for a richer bloom and provides more food for krill and feeder fish."

He stood and wrapped the towel around his hips. "Then life in the ocean would die without mermaids?"

"No, of course not. We simply make it more plentiful."

"Interesting. Are you hungry?"

"Now that you mention it…"

"I think I have something you'll like. Good thing I stopped by the grocery store on my way here this afternoon." He headed for the door.

Draya waited for the painful sense of separation she'd suffered earlier when he left to fix the power, but it didn't happen. As he clanked dishes, opened and closed doors, and made appliances hum in the kitchen, the hail gave way to a heavy but quieter downpour. A chill she hadn't noticed while laying next to Gavin's heat made her shiver and she folded the covers and climbed under.

The warm linens relaxed her. Resting the side of her face on the pillow, she closed her eyes and tried to figure out what had caused her to wash onto the rocks. Lindee had shrieked as magic yanked her through the waves after that ship. The ocean had pitched and rolled, but nothing worse than she'd experienced before.

Had she been so focused on her sister she'd missed a tidal surge? Impossible. She would've sensed it. What had taken her unawares? What had pushed her onto the rocks?

A mouthwatering aroma stirred her hunger. The fragrance, rich and full, filled her senses and made her swallow in anticipation.

"Are you asleep?" whispered Gavin from the doorway.

"No." She sat as he came in carrying two bowls, their steaming contents strengthening the delicious smell. He wore dark blue sweatpants but no shirt. She admired the lines of his well-formed body. "I was trying to remember how I'd gotten tossed onto the rocks."

"Any luck?"

"No. It was dark and chaotic, and I just can't put the pieces together."

He came and settled on the edge of the bed then handed her a bowl. "Give it time. I'm sure it'll come to you."

"Aren't you going to join me?" Draya patted a spot next to her hip.

"I don't want to crowd you."

"You won't crowd me. I like being close to you."

"I'll just sit here. I hope you like clam chowder." He spooned some between his lips.

Her stomach gurgled but she ignored it. *Did I do something wrong? Say something wrong?* She studied him, realizing he appeared much calmer than before they'd made love. In fact, all her pain had fled, too. She touched a finger to her head injury and it didn't hurt.

"How is it?" he asked, his gaze on her hand as it came from her hair.

"Almost back to normal."

He smiled and shook his head. "Amazing."

"You know what I think is amazing?"

"What?"

"You."

Chapter Six

Why do you have to be so beautiful, so interesting? You'll leave in the morning and I'll be devastated. God help him, he'd fallen in love with her.

The storm that had gentled for a bit renewed its strength and crashed through the night. Yet it didn't bother him. A clap of thunder shook the house but it didn't shake his nerves. Draya had done something mystical to him, and he wasn't complaining.

She took a bite of chowder and arched her brows. "Yum. This is marvelous."

"Thanks. Tell me about singing whales into migration. What does that mean?" Maybe if he understood her better, he could convince her to stay.

"The whales go south to have their babies. It's easier down there since the waters are clear and there aren't as many predators. Less food equals fewer sharks and no giant squid. The problem is, there's not much food for the mamas, either. They have to nurse their young and teach them about the ocean while not getting enough to eat. By the time their babies are strong and can migrate north, the mamas are thin and tired. It's a scary time."

"And singing helps?"

"Yes. We meet them a hundred miles farther down the coast. The supply of food is good there and the mamas always stop. Whales are great parents, but when they're starving, they do what they have to. So for a week, we take the calves for a few hours each day so the mothers can dive deep and take advantage of the ready food."

"You baby sit."

Draya released a breathy laugh. "Yes. We whale-baby sit. Then we sing the mamas along. It's a song we pass from mother to daughter, a whale song that reminds the mamas about the bounty and comfort of cooler northern waters. We accompany them here and sing them farewell as they continue."

He tried to imagine it, but had difficulty. "Why do the mother whales trust you with their young?"

She shrugged slender shoulders and clutched the sheet to her chest. "They remember us from previous years, and from when they were babies. Whales never forget."

"Like elephants?"

"I don't know anything about elephants."

Right. No elephants in the ocean. Gavin scraped his bowl and spooned the last of the chowder into his mouth. Before he stood, however, a streak of lightning screamed in the night, filling the room with a shock of light at the same time a thunder boomer threatened to deafen him. The power blinked out.

Damn it.

"Gavin?"

"I'm right here."

A series of flashes illuminated her frightened features.

He took her half eaten chowder and stacked it on his empty bowl before putting them on the floor. Scooting closer, he gathered her into his arms. He loved the protectiveness she inspired. "Are you afraid of the dark?"

She pressed her forehead against the side of his neck and hugged her arms around him. "No. It's dark at the bottom of the sea."

"Then what is it?" He stroked her hair, liking the way her curls caressed his fingers. He couldn't get over how good she smelled.

"The noise."

"I get that. The noise scares a lot of people and I imagine we have a lot more loud, startling noises here on land than you've had in the water."

"Stay with me," she said and squeezed him sweetly.

"I'm not going anywhere."

* * * *

Draya awoke with a start, the images of her dream still vivid in her mind. While sleeping, she relived surfacing in the storm. Lindee had followed her calling, then Draya had gone to the rocks.

"I wasn't tossed," she said in disbelief, sitting and blinking.

Gavin sat and brushed her hair over her shoulder, studying her face. "What do you mean?"

"Onto the rocks." She turned and stared with a new perspective at the man who had changed her life in a single night. "I wasn't tossed. I was pulled."

He shook his head. "I'm still not following."

Running the events of the night through her head, she said, "Think about it. When you were shouting in the storm, was it just in fear or was there pain?"

"There has always been pain of heartache over what I did to my sister." He furrowed his brows. "You know what? You're right. It was different. More like a breaking heart than guilt."

"I felt it, too. I just *had* to go to you. I thought it was to help because you were shouting and might be hurt, but the urge was so strong it got me out of bed and nearly to the front door when I was still too ill to be up. And how about when you wanted to leave to get a condom?"

He rubbed his chin. "Yeah, that was definitely weird. But that pain was worse. Like a knife stabbed me between the eyes, and something was pulling my heart out."

"I felt that, too. Do you see?"

He gave a solemn nod. "You're saying you got your calling to your life-mate."

"The magic pulled me out of the ocean and onto those rocks." She couldn't believe it. Finally. And to a human, like her sister. "You're my life-mate."

"*I'm* your life-mate?" A slow smile brightened his features and put a sparkle in his eyes.

"What did you think? Why would you feel the pain of parting if you weren't linked to me?" She kissed his cheek.

His smile melted. "Oh, geez. Does this mean we can never be out of each other's sight without that pain?"

She laughed. "No. It's only that way until the physical bond has been met. We bonded last night—your body to mine. Your heart to mine."

"Your soul to mine." He stared at her, his eyes wide with realization. "I'm your life-mate. You're my *soul* mate."

"I am?" Soul mates. It sounded perfect. She smiled.

"You really are. I've been laying here holding you while you slept, listening to the nor'easter blow over, and I've suddenly got all these ideas for books. I haven't had a single idea since my first one, but now with you, I've got six."

"Six. Wow."

"Wow is right." He searched her face with a look of wonderment. "You're amazing, Draya."

He pressed his lips to hers. With exhilarating joy, she threw her arms around his neck and drowned in his kiss and all it meant—love, acceptance, forever.

As she came out of her euphoria, the quiet in the house closed in on her. "The storm. It's over."

"It blew past about half an hour ago." He swept curls from her forehead.

From the window, gray morning light spilled across the floor. Waves lapped against the rocky shore with a hushed but unmistakable hiss of spray. She could still smell the electrical charge left in the air by the storm. Or was it between Gavin and her? She grinned.

In the distance, the steady thumping of a ship's engine grew louder.

Lindee! She sensed her sister grow near. Leaping from the bed, she cried, "I have to go outside."

"What is it?" Gavin jumped for the edge of the bed. "Are you leaving me?"

She froze. "No, I'm not leaving. Lindee's coming." She stepped into his sweatpants and tied the string at her bellybutton. "I have to go see for myself that she's okay."

"Wait for me. I'll come with you." He stalked from the room while she pulled her halter over her head.

She touched the place where her injury had caused such an ache the night before, but the bump had smoothed and a thin scab promised to disappear by midday.

In the living room, Gavin had a suitcase open on the couch. He wore a pair of gray sweatpants and shrugged into a white T-shirt. "What about your father? Didn't you say he'd worry if you don't return?"

She shook her head. "You're my life-mate. I was called to you. He'll know. He won't expect me back."

"I guess it's one of those mermaid things I'll never understand." Holding out a hand, he asked, "Ready?"

Draya took his hand, and with her heart in her throat, rushed from the house. He led her to the grassy slope overlooking the sea where whitecaps and swells appeared shockingly normal compared to the turbulent violence that had thrown them together. Around the corner of the point, a merchant ship headed out of the shipping channel and toward deep ocean. A movement on the top deck caught her attention.

Lindee stood in the arms of a tall man with pale hair, and she waved wildly at Draya. Even at such a distance, she looked content. Happy.

Draya waved and settled back against Gavin as he wrapped strong arms around her. "She's found her future."

"So have you," he whispered close to her ear. "I hope you're up for a challenge."

She laughed and turned in his arms. "I'm always up for an adventure."

"Well, you found a lifelong one." He kissed her with a passion that sealed their bond. "Draya, stay."

"Forever, my love. Forever."

The End

Sea Angel
By Laura Kitchell

A mermaid faces a painful death if she cannot find her calling and mate within the hour. The only male in the area is a sea-angel, the one creature who can rob her of gills and tail with a single touch. Will she die alone, having never known passion's bliss? Or can she risk his touch and take the chance of drowning in his arms?

To Catch A Dream
(In the Merlicious Digest, or single)

Sargo, a mermaid princess, must convince Paul, a human, that he's a merman, a king, and he has to marry her.

You can email Laura at lkitchell@exis.net

Sea Angel
By Laura Kitchell

Chapter One

"Please, Father. Anyone. I don't care." It wasn't true. Brandine *did* care, but when pain gripped her and refused to let go, she cared less.

"I won't bond you to just anyone. You're my daughter. I know you're in heat and it hurts, but we have time. At least a day." He turned his massive back on her and filled a fancy stein with heavy octopus oil from a barnacle-encrusted pitcher. Dark tendrils of oil escaped and curled in the saltwater before dissipating.

"But—"

"No!" he bellowed. "I've already lost two of my daughters this afternoon to *humans*, of all creatures. The gods play their games with Draya and Lindee, but they won't have their way with you. Not you, Brandine." He took a long draw from the stein then wiped black oil sticking to his mustache with the back of his hand.

She jutted her chin. *Tyrant*. "How do you know my sisters were called to humans?" And what was so bad about it?

"Never you mind. I know and that should be good enough for you."

"I don't believe in your gods, Father. There's only one God. When you realize the truth Mother so faithfully taught us, perhaps He will stop punishing you."

His eyes softened. "I loved your mother, but she had some strange ideas. I love you, too, Daughter. Now go. I have work to do if I'm to find a life-mate who deserves you." Clunking the stein on a thick wooden table, he caused more tendrils of oil to waft into the water. He swam toward the other end of the chamber, mumbling thoughtfully. "Maybe Prince Tarman. I heard he hasn't found a life-mate yet, either."

Talking to him sometimes seemed the same as talking to a hammerhead shark—neither had any interest in what she had to say, both would do exactly what they wanted, regardless, and she wasted her time trying. Brandine gave a powerful swish of her tail and hastened out between stone pillars surrounding the shipwreck her father called home. She headed for the broken section of pilothouse she'd once shared with her sisters but now had to herself. She didn't like the aloneness.

A cramp tightened a fist in her abdomen and she stopped. The fist yanked her insides. She grunted, doubling over as a tiny bit of blood drizzled from her tail slit. The bleeding had begun. Her stomach dropped with dread. She didn't have a day like her father thought.

The fist loosened then yanked again. Whimpering, she squeezed her eyes closed and curled into a ball. She expected to settle to the silt floor, but a swift current swept down and scooped her along. Despite being a strong swimmer, Brandine couldn't evade the water's clutch. She balled in pain, helpless.

Swirls of rushing current whipped her hair, letting her know she moved fast, but she didn't open her eyes until the cramp ended. The flow released her as quickly as it has snatched her, and she drifted in residual propulsion from her strange ride. Unable to make out her surroundings in an unusually dark sea, she shot to the surface to see if she could gain her bearings by the stars.

Zeet!

Lightning zigzagged, striking the water with a sizzle and blinding her. Jerking in alarm, she slapped a hand over her racing heart. An enormous swell tossed her high then a cresting wave slammed her under. Gasping and blinking, she tumbled through buffeting top-water and fought for the deep. The ocean refused her access, pressing her to the surface again and again as she continued to struggle for long minutes to recapture control and break from the turbulent storm-ravaged waves. It took the last of her strength.

Once she passed into calmer layers, she went limp and sank to the bottom of the ocean hoping cooler water beneath the thermal layer would refresh her. It didn't. Another cramp grasped her about the waist and squeezed away her ability to breathe.

She opened her mouth on a silent scream as a rush of blood floated past her face in a blossom of red, twisting like a flower before melting into the gentle current stirring the sand around her. Sharp pain came next, making her writhe wildly like a fish out of water. The cramp let up enough for her to gulp a breath then wrung her as though she were a wet washcloth.

This time, she managed to scream before losing the function of her lungs.

* * * *

Kyleal popped a palm against his ear. He was hearing things. Resting his head on his arm, he squirmed deeper into a nest of downy linens he'd discovered in a sunken ship and stared at glowing deep-sea snails that lit the ceiling of his cozy cave. The storm surely played havoc with the currents because he'd never heard them shriek that way.

A low moan drifted by the cave opening. He rolled to his side and lifted his head. Next to the stone shelf he used as a bed, the silt floor shifted and two eyes blinked at him.

"Don't look at me like that, Flea. It's just the storm."

The eyes blinked again.

"I'm serious. There's nobody for miles. That's why I chose this place to live, remember?"

With attitude, his pet fluke flung sand at him, closed its lids and wiggled from under its cover. It swam outside.

Kyleal sighed. "Fine. If it'll make you feel better, I'll check it out." He sat and stretched, combing toes through soft sand. Adjusting his pelvic fin to ensure modesty, just in case, he flexed the huge dorsal fin attached to his spine to gain buoyancy then kicked his legs.

Webbing between his toes propelled him past the mild eddy at the entrance, and he shifted his useless, wing-like pectoral fins so they floated behind rather than into his face. To keep them from drifting forward, he clamped his elbows to his sides, pinning the base of the fins just below his armpits.

Compared with the luminescence in his home, the darkness from the storm gave him pause. With irritation, he flicked a wayward pectoral fin that came forward, despite his precaution, and brushed his cheek while he waited for his eyes to adjust.

A flash of bright green caught his attention. Going horizontal, he swam to investigate. Something large listlessly rolled in the current that caressed the ocean floor. Cautiously, he approached, ready to fight in case a predator lay in wait. He racked his brain to think of any with the flashing green of a mahi-mahi. Not a single one came to mind.

He glanced at the glowing entrance to his cave. Maybe he should go get some of the snails to light his way. A soft whimper brought him around. Squinting, he twitched his dorsal fin to get closer. Did he see correctly? He rubbed his eyes.

A mermaid lolled in the silt, her eyes closed and her body limp.

"Hello?"

Her eyes flew open—dark eyes for a mermaid. Rare. He couldn't tell their color in the storm shadows, but they were large in her delicately featured face.

"Sea-angel," she whispered, as if she didn't believe what she saw.

He hated that name for his species. "I prefer to be called a krispin." How would she like it if he called her a fish-woman? "What's wrong with you? Why are you just lying there?"

"I'm dying." She closed her eyes.

He found that hard to believe. She appeared peaceful, sleeping. Unable to take his gaze from her lovely countenance, he hung above and waited for her to rouse.

"Go away," she murmured, still not moving as she inched along in the water's flow.

"Why are you dying?"

Opening her eyes, she scowled at him. "What do you care? You should be off seducing every krispin female you can get your hands on. Isn't that what you do?"

Now, there was a show of life. He liked her irascibility. "Misconception. A krispin male doesn't live solely to mate." Though he had friends who acted that way.

She sniffed disdainfully and rolled, closing her eyes. "Stop staring at me."

"Why don't you swim home?"

She ignored him.

"Wake up." *You're no fun when you just lie there.*

"Please leave me alone."

Please? Maybe something really was wrong. "Tell me why you think you're dying."

"I don't *think* I'm dying. I *am* dying. Now, please leave."

"No. I want to know why." He loved a good puzzle, and she presented the best mystery he'd ever run across.

"Then you'll have to suffer in your curiosity."

Stubborn mermaid. No. More like crazy mermaid. Crossing his arms over his chest, he went vertical and stared at her for a moment. She began to lose her entertainment value.

The fluke arrived and nudged her hip.

"Fine. See if you can get an interesting response out of her, Flea. I give up. I'm going home." He headed for his cave, glancing at her from time to time, but she never moved.

He swam into his home but didn't settle on the bed as he'd planned. He stared unseeing at a fading Oriental rug he'd hung on the stone wall behind his bed, unable to get her gorgeous face out of his mind. She really was a lovely creature, from what he could tell in the dark. It'd be a shame if she died.

Using only his dorsal fin, he paced. He hadn't noticed any injuries. She wore the smooth lines of youth in her features, so she wasn't dying of old age. Perhaps she had a disease.

Flea scuttled in and settled on his bed.

"No luck, huh?"

The fluke fluttered the edges of its ridge fins with agitation.

"What do you want me to do?" demanded Kyleal. "She told me to leave her alone." So why couldn't he forget about her?

A scream severed his thoughts.

"That sounded bad." He rushed from the cave as a bolt of lightning stabbed the water above. The light revealed the mermaid balled inside a pink haze.

He raced toward her as she released another scream. Before he reached her, he smelled what surrounded her.

Blood.

Chapter Two

"Where did it get you? Was it a shark?" The sea-angel's deep, worried voice pulled Brandine out of her pain-induced trance.

"I thought you left," she forced past a throat tight with agony, refusing to open her eyes.

"What the hell is wrong with you?"

Why was *he* angry? And why did he care? The pain subsided and she wiped oily tears to clear her vision. "I'm dying. Isn't that enough wrongness for you?"

He swayed from side to side, searching her. "I don't see the wound. What's all this blood? Where are you hurt?"

Despite the last bout of pain, she'd regained some strength. She placed a hand on the ocean floor to stop her momentum in the current and sat. "For an angel, you sure are giving me a devil of a time."

His wings rose high, rippling delicately in the moving water behind his head. Even in the gray light, his curls appeared pale. He had strong, angular features and piercing eyes. She couldn't quite discern their color. Like an angel suspended in descent, he held his arms out, one knee slightly bent, and gazed upon her from his vertical height. The krispin was male beauty at its best.

"I'm not an angel." He glowered.

"That much is becoming increasingly clear." What would it take to get the curious creature to leave her alone? He was great to look at, but he got on her nerves. Couldn't a dying mermaid have some peace in her last hours?

He sneered. "Are you going to tell me why you're dying?"

"No. It's nothing you can help me with. I'm lost. There's no one near who can save me, and I've given up hope." Had she? Pushing off the sand, she found her balance and glanced around. Where should she go?

"So you don't *have* to die?" He moved closer. Behind him, the filmy wing-like membranes gently waved and lent him a gracefulness at perfect odds with the sheer strength exuding from every line of his body.

Fury over the injustice of her impending painful death and anger at his persistence sent her into a rage. It built, heating her face and forming a knot in her stomach. With a powerful swish of her tail, she charged him. Speeding past, careful not to make contact, she pushed a wall of water that shoved him hard.

"All you do is ask questions!" She spun to face him. Pointing an accusing finger, she said, "You treat me like a freak. Like I'm here as a cure for your boredom. You're pathetic." *And beautiful.* "You're the freak, out here by yourself so far from shore and others of your kind." *And if you were a merman, I'd beg you to take me.*

He recovered, giving his head a vigorous shake. "All I did was ask you a question."

She planted a fist on her hip. "All you *do* is ask questions."

"You're wrong, by the way." The corner of his mouth quirked in a half smile, but his eyes held a profound sadness.

"Oh, yeah? About what?" *I need to stop staring at his sexy, kissable lips.*

"I'm not far from shore." He pointed toward a long line of rocky outcropping. "We're ten miles out in forty feet of water."

What? Brandine glanced up, trying to discern the wavering barrier between water temperatures. She couldn't. Even in the shadows cast by the storm, she could tell no thermal layer existed. "But that means I'm a hundred miles from home." How was that possible? It explained why cooler waters hadn't eased her pain. There *weren't* any.

"Afraid so. Now will you talk to me?"

Her senses whirled. Magic was at work. No way could she have traveled a hundred miles in minutes. "Talk? I've probably only got a few hours to live, and you want to talk?"

He inched closer. "You said you could be helped. How? What's killing you?" He glanced around as if searching for a threat.

Real hopelessness overwhelmed her. Averting her gaze in shame, she whispered, "I'm in heat." If he laughed, she'd make him pay…somehow.

He didn't. Tilting his head slightly, he asked, "Where's your mate?"

Oh, God, I'm really not going to make it. I don't want to die. "I haven't been called."

The light faded further and thunder found its way through the ocean in a muffled rumble.

He went utterly still. His expression changed, but she couldn't read it. "Well, I'm not going to bond with you."

Her jaw dropped. "I didn't ask you to." *Out of the question.*

He raked her with his stare. "If I bonded with you, I'd be stuck with you following me everywhere."

"I didn't *ask* you to," she said with indignation. "Krispins don't lifemate. You're always looking for the next female, for something better to come along. I wouldn't *have* you, even if we could." Though the longer she stared at him, the more he appealed to her.

No, stop. It was just her desperation making him seem appealing. And her state of heat. And his graceful, sensual presence. And the way he made her feel like the most important female in the ocean when he stared. *No, stop.*

One touch from him would make her take human form. She'd drown without her gills. Definitely *not* appealing.

"What makes you think we can't? What are your options, mermaid?"

The nearest mer-colony was probably fifty miles. At her healthiest, it would've taken over an hour to get that far. With debilitating cramps and intensifying pain slowing and stopping her, she wouldn't make it. Some mermaids had made homes close to shore, as her sister, Draya, had a couple years ago, but mermen never did.

She studied the rock ridge. "You said we're ten miles from shore?"

"Yes. So?"

A human. Maybe the magic had brought her close to shore to bond with a human. The instant she thought it, she realized it wasn't so. Bonding magic didn't work that way. She would be drawn to shore against her will. Pulled by force to her life-mate. But surely she could find a man to bond with, though. Her father could go spit.

* * * *

"I see what you're thinking. Go ahead. Good luck with that." Kyleal gave her a dismissive wave. If she preferred a stinky, hairy, clumsy human to him, then she deserved whatever she found.

As she swam toward shore, disappearing quickly into the murkiness the storm created, he couldn't convince himself to return to the cave. Flea bumped his foot. Ignoring his pet, he stared at the space where she'd gone out of sight.

Did he expect her to come back? Did he think she would change her mind and come swimming into his arms? He was a fool.

He didn't *want* her to come back. Why would he want a mermaid bonded to him? He'd break her heart when he went philandering, and *all* krispins played the population. She had it right. He was no exception.

With a sigh, he meandered home. A stabbing headache made him cringe. *So much for a relaxing evening.*

She had him interested and intrigued. What would happen? Would she find a human to bond with? What would become of her? He was anything but bored. In fact, he had to fight the urge to follow.

Flea followed, and at the cave entrance, brushed against his leg.

"I'm not going after her." Kyleal jerked his foot to discourage the fluke from taking another run at him. "I didn't see *you* go swimming to her aid when she screamed. Coward."

The fluke turned its caudal fin to him and sank to the silt.

"Be that way." Kyleal went inside and reclined on his bed. He ran fingertips through the fibrous yarn of carpet on the wall. After the excitement and heated exchange with the feisty mermaid, however, he couldn't summon any interest in watching snails creep across the ceiling. He raked an anxious hand through his hair.

Maybe he should take her advice and go find a female krispin who'd offer bed-sport for the night. He sat and stared at the dark cave opening. He scooted to the edge of the stone shelf, causing the bedding to bunch.

But he didn't go.

The mermaid was right. He *was* a freak. Krispin males adored the docility of krispin females, but he didn't. His friends had no problem finding a new lover when they grew bored, but he despised the constant courtship the lifestyle required. And krispin males didn't care when their lovers sought beds of other males, but he did.

So if he didn't want a krispin female and the meaningless fling she could only offer, what *did* he want?

"Ugh!" Kyleal heaved off the bed. Needing to release some nervous energy, he rolled into a somersault at the center of the cave. "Don't think you're sneaking. I saw you slither in here under the sand."

A flounder-shaped outline shuddered near the wall then two eyelids slid back. Flea blinked at him once.

"Stare all you want. You're not going to make me feel guilty for letting her go. What am I supposed to do with a mermaid? I may be done with casual sex…for now…but I don't want a wife, either. And definitely not a mermaid wife." He sliced an angry arm through the water. "We krispins like a life that's quiet and predictable. A mermaid would have me all over the place. Hundreds of miles into deep ocean, swimming with dolphins and whales, hunting giant squid with her father…who probably wouldn't like me anyway. No way!"

He crossed arms over his chest and scowled. Flea blinked expectantly.

"Okay, okay. So maybe some of it would be fun." He'd never suffer boredom with a mermaid—that he *knew* for sure.

He shook his head. "Krispins don't mate for life. It's just not in us. I'd wind up cheating on her and she'd be heartbroken. Stuck with me because of the bond and hating the fact that she loves me."

What did he just say? Could a mermaid love him? Hell, could anything love him?

A scream, distant but unmistakable, echoed along the current that ran past his cave.

Flea swam for the exit but Kyleal torpedoed past. That mermaid needed him whether she liked it or not.

Chapter Three

Too shallow. Too close to the storm.
Brandine panted through the agony of a stifling cramp and the anguish of losing her life—a life she hadn't lived to the fullest. Nearly constant flashes from the sky lit the sea. She hadn't made it to shore, and now she huddled at an eighteen-foot depth as the warmer shallow water leeched blood from her body. Thunder rumbled, vibrating the ocean around her.

Shivering with the unfamiliar sensation, she clawed the strange, rocky floor trying to get to a small cavern-like crevice in the ridge. At the corner of her vision, she caught a stalking gray mass warily moving her way. Strobe light bounced through the violently shifting surface and reflected off rock and shell faces, making it impossible to distinguish an exact shape. She was certain of one thing, though. It was a shark.

Her heart banged against her ribs as she scrabbled for safety. Before she could drag her seizing body into the recess, pain like a knife sliced her from pelvis to sternum. It paralyzed her.

The water went to red around her and the shark jerked with excitement. It shot in a straight line over her, sending the bloody water swirling. Curving around, it came at her. Releasing a shaky sob, she waited for its sharp teeth. This was not how she had imagined dying.

Something went past so fast it blurred. Brandine blinked, and when she looked, the shark had veered. It circled around and came in for another try. Above the shark, the sea-angel dove with tremendous speed and thumped the beast on the head. It thrashed side-to-side then changed course and sailed over her.

Like a being from heaven, the krispin went vertical and floated to her, his arms stretched outward, one leg extended downward, and his wings fluttering delicately through the water. Without a word, he reached for her.

"No! Don't touch me." The shark would have been bad, but drowning would be worse—the worst possible death for a mermaid. Not the way she wanted to die.

"Why not?"

"Aaaa"! The knife cut into her.

"You're going to bleed to death." He came closer.

Thrusting out a staying hand, she said through clenched teeth, "I'll drown. Don't do it."

"Misconception." He squatted.

"Don't."

"Stop me." He slipped an arm under her shoulders and another behind her knees. Human knees.

Oh, God. She held her breath.

Clutching her close, he shoved from the floor and swam along the rock ridge into deeper water. "You can breathe," he whispered in her ear.

I can't.

"Don't ignore me, beautiful. Breathe."

I can't! Her chest began to burn and she grabbed his shoulder. *I can't.*

Surprised, she released the oxygen-reduced water from her lungs. *This is it. I'll be dead in a minute and I've never known the hands of a lover.* A terrible sadness clogged her throat and she drew water in on a shuddering breath.

"That's right. Breathe."

She breathed? She breathed! She released the water and drew more through gills that still existed and worked. "How did you know?" she asked, her words slurring a bit.

He cleared his throat. "That's not important. You're alive and out of harm's way. That's what matters."

"Out of harm's way? Have you *not* been paying attention? I'd guess I don't even have an hour left. I've lost so much blood I can barely move."

"Then there's only one thing left to do."

"You swim fast, but I don't think you could get me a hundred miles into mer-territory in time. It's over, krispin. If I've accepted it, you have to, too."

* * * *

Like hell. Kyleal didn't have to accept her death, and he wouldn't. "You're not going to die. I won't let that happen."

She whimpered. "You don't have a choice." Her body stiffening in his arms, she turned her face into his chest and released a silent scream. Her fingers dug into his shoulder as an alarming amount of blood rushed from between her legs.

His heart skipped a beat then thudded with horrified dread. He had to hurry. She might not like his solution, but *she* had no choice. Increasing his speed, he left lightning-pale waters for storm-darkened depths.

Flea swam at them and landed on her curled stomach.

In pitch-blackness that now consumed the sea, a soft glow let him know when he approached his cave. Hugging her tighter, he said, "Hold on, mermaid. We're almost there."

Flea fluttered off her and swam for a raised pile of sand near the entrance as Kyleal crested the ridge and went inside. Gently, he lighted on the bed with the mermaid on his lap. He didn't want to let her go.

She relaxed in his arms, releasing her death-grip on his shoulder, and turned to rest her cheek against him. "I want to live."

"I want you to live."

"Why?"

He didn't know. Pressing a kiss to the top of her head, he closed his eyes and savored the caress of her silky red hair settling over his shoulder and down his back. Red. The glow of the snails gave it a fiery quality. He wouldn't have guessed. Even in the lightning bright waters near shore, it had appeared orange-brown. He much preferred this color.

He had to see her eyes. With a finger under her chin, he urged her to look at him. Long lashes brushed her cheeks a moment before she opened big eyes the color of a king's purple tail. Magnificent. He stared into their darkness, noticing flecks of lavender sparkling at the edges like perfect amethysts.

"I've never seen eyes the color of yours," he said. He could stare into them for days and not grow bored.

"Me, neither. I'm the only one I know with this color." She lowered her gaze then glanced around the cave. "This is where you live?"

"Yes." He braced for criticism.

"I thought krispins lived in cities and shared homes. You live alone?"

"I'm not like other krispins." He grimaced.

"I'm learning that."

Swallowing hard, he hated that her opinion meant something to him. "I guess I really am the freak you said I am."

"You risked your life to save me from that shark. I can't think you're anything but brave and wonderful. An angel."

He cringed. "I really don't like that nickname for our species."

She turned innocently seductive eyes on him. "I didn't call you a sea-angel. I said *you're* an angel. My guardian angel."

His chest swelled against his will. "Where's that feisty mermaid who refused to answer my questions and give me any satisfaction?"

"I'm sorry, krispin. I'm done. I've got no more fight left in me." A heavy tear dripped over her lid, lingered a moment on her lashes, then evaporated into the saltwater in an oily wisp.

He'd put the fight back in her. Lowering her shoulders, he bent and placed his lips to hers. He waited for her to resist, but she didn't. Her fingers found his shoulder once more, but this time, they landed with a light reluctance. Confused, he pulled away and studied her peaceful face. Why didn't she push him away?

"Do that again," she said.

"Why?"

"Because it makes the pain stop."

It did? He touched his mouth to hers and sighed when she moved her hand from his shoulder to the side of his neck. His stomach quivering, he added pressure. She shifted on his lap, turning to him and sliding her other hand under his arm. Her halter-encased breasts rubbed against his chest while her fingers grazed the base of his pectoral fin where it connected. A thrill unlike anything he'd experienced tore through him, setting his blood on fire.

Under his pressure, she opened. She touched her tongue to his. The gesture was sweet and hesitant. It stole his ability to think and sent a shockwave of awareness through his entire being. It shook him.

He broke the kiss and searched her glistening eyes. Who was this mermaid? She couldn't be just any mermaid. "Wow," he said, blown away by the protective need she inspired.

"What?" she whispered, a slight smile softening her mouth.

"You." He'd never had so much desire for anything, for anyone. With a wave of his dorsal fin, he lifted off the bed. He pivoted and laid her on the bedding, keeping hold of one hand. "You're so beautiful."

Her long red hair flowed over the edge of the shelf and her slender, shapely curves far exceeded the charms any female krispin could boast. The mermaid's flawless, pale skin shone in the gentle glow from the ceiling, and her eyes seemed enormous compared with the fine features of her face. She lowered lashes to her cheeks, and Kyleal took advantage to get a good look at the rest of her graceful body.

His shaft hardened at the sight of high, firm breasts rounding at the top of her halter. A hint of ribs under white skin rippled to a dainty waist. The slightest curve of belly below her bellybutton led his gaze to the juncture between her firm thighs. Stirrings like nothing he'd felt before made modesty behind his pelvic fin impossible. He moved it aside, flattening it to his hip.

"Kyleal," he said.

She opened her eyes, her gaze meeting with his vitals. He hardened painfully.

"Kyleal?" she asked.

"My name. It's Kyleal."

She smiled, showing straight white teeth between kiss-reddened lips. "Kyleal. You're going to save me, aren't you?"

"Yes." The word was ripped from him, as if it came from his heart rather than his throat.

Chapter Four

Brandine's heart hammered a rapid tattoo. He wasn't a merman or a human. No, he was the most stunning display of male virility she'd ever seen. Looking at him made her eyes want to cross with need. "How did you know I wouldn't drown?"

"My father."

She tried to wrap her mind around those two words. "Your father mated with a mermaid?" Could it be?

He shrugged. "I don't know how he knew."

In the light of the cave, she realized he had the palest blue eyes. Blond curls with light brown depths swept from his forehead and went into a sexy riot behind his ears and at a strong neck. Broad shoulders graduated to muscular arms—the arms that had rescued her from a shark and carried her to the safety of his home. Arms she wanted holding her.

His chest proclaimed his might with two slabs of thick muscle above a rippled abdomen. His straining member promised a life-giving bonding the likes she would never forget. At either side, sinew and muscle encased narrow hips. And with bulging evidence of his strength creating amazing lines on his long legs, she understood how he'd achieved such tremendous speed while fighting the shark. Speed any merman would be proud to possess. She itched to touch him.

Adjusting his buoyancy, he moved above her, hovering a moment before covering her body with his. She welcomed him with open arms.

"Brandine," she said, staring into his blue eyes and combing fingers into his curls.

"Your name is Brandine?"

"Yes."

His gaze found her mouth. "It's as lovely as you."

"Thank you." She skimmed a hand along his ribs and located the base of his pectoral fin below his armpit. The silken feel fascinated her, and she brushed fingertips along it.

He inhaled sharply, letting her know he liked it. His rigid shaft grazed her thigh as he settled between them. Moisture rushed from between her legs, and this time, it wasn't blood.

"How much foreplay do you prefer?" he asked with a tight, deep voice.

"None," she whispered. "This isn't for fun. This is my life."

"Your life," he said on a groan, fitting his tip to her opening. "You're so ready."

"Yes. Take me."

He sent his tip through her slick, oily juices, once up through her folds and down, then entered her in a single thrust.

They both cried out.

Brandine shuddered as pleasure rocked her unawares, blanking her mind and infusing her with a flood of energy. Drawing a long gulp of water through her gills, she arched against Kyleal. She couldn't get close enough.

He withdrew and plunged. Her walls trembled around him. In her chest, her lungs labored and her heart called out to his. He withdrew and thrust, again and again. Meeting each thrust with a tilt of her hips, she strove for the ultimate connection. She needed this. She needed him. God help her, she needed his love.

He didn't stop. He set a rhythm that matched the pounding of her heartbeat. With the tenderness she craved, he placed a kiss to her lips and removed her halter. His movement caressed his chest across her nipples, heightening her pleasure and creating an electric charge deep in her very core.

It built gradually, with each jut of his hips, each brush of his chest. He cupped her jaw and urged her to open. His tongue entered her mouth, beginning a sensuous dance with hers that entranced her and made the walls of her passage quake.

She hugged him tightly, suspended over the chasm of release.

Breaking from the kiss, he locked gazes with her and joined her at the edge of the abyss. "Come with me," he said, his voice thick and his eyes swirling with passion.

"Come to me," she answered.

Wrapping awkward legs around his hips, she took him deep. Together, they tumbled into the great unknown. She clung to him, her heart pressed to his, her cheek to the side of his neck. She fell into weightless nothingness until she shattered, her pieces mingling with his, becoming one being with him. For a time, they formed something new and wonderful and unique. Not him. Not her. Them.

She jerked on a pained gasp, her essence separating from his. She emerged with her life renewed. Joy and vitality washed over her in waves. Delight filling every void that had ever existed, she pressed her lips to his jaw and loosed her legs from around him.

"Thank you."

* * * *

No! Kyleal reeled. What just happened? He wasn't himself and then he was. Horrified, he pulled free of her body and bolted from the bed. His mind whirled, trying to make sense of the foreign yearning that tugged at his very being, the way his heart felt swollen, the way orgasm had hurt *after* release. It wasn't supposed to hurt.

This is my life, she had said.

Pointing an accusing finger, he demanded, "What did you do?"

Sadness pulled the corners of her eyes. "I didn't do it. *You* did. You bonded me to you."

The bonding. Magic. Was that what had yanked him into a cosmic void and mixed him into a mess? And why did his body tingle? Why couldn't he look at her? Oh, God, what had he done?

"Kyleal?"

He shook his head and held up a hand. Fitting his pelvic fin into a modest position, he shook. He needed to run. To swim as fast as he could and never look back. He didn't understand this terrifying desire overwhelming him. Not desire for sex. Not desire for excitement. Desire for something he couldn't name, something he didn't comprehend.

"I have to go," he said. "I'm sorry."

He raced from the cave, barely noticing Flea emerge from his sand pile. Fear surged through his veins, fueling his flight and taking him to a speed he'd never achieved. With his heart ready to burst, he raced for the sky. He shot past the surface and hit air with a shout.

Spreading his pectoral fins over his outstretched arms, he flew on an updraft and silently begged the storm to strike him down. "Hit me!" he yelled at a bolt of lightning.

Thunder clapped his answer. *Suffer!*

"Aaaaaa!"

Did he somehow offend God? Was he destined for a life of suffering and fear for what he had done with Brandine? Had Kyleal interfered with God's design for her time to die? He slammed into the waves and lay there, staring at the flashing black clouds as the turbulent sea pitched him this way and that.

Everything ached. His body. His heart. His *soul*.

He closed his eyes, but all he could see was Brandine's gorgeous face. Her sweet voice echoed in his ears. His body remembered and craved hers.

"No!" His scream reverberated off cresting waves.

He couldn't have her. He didn't deserve her. Covering his face with his hands, he rode the buffeting ocean.

She had tried to tell him. She had asked him to leave her alone, had begged him not to touch her. Why didn't he listen? *He* was the stubborn one.

He had known better. A krispin and a mermaid? Unheard of.

"I'm a fool," he yelled into the night. "I'm a fool," he whispered.

He couldn't go back. She had her tail now…and her life. She could go anywhere and do anything. Flinging his arms wide, he grabbed at the water. *She's bonded to me. She won't.*

She probably thought she loved him. Didn't she realize he was incapable of love? If he went to the cave, he'd find her waiting. He wouldn't do that to her. She had to figure out eventually that he wouldn't return. She'd be free then. Wouldn't she?

Where should he go when all he wanted was to return to his home? Return to *her*.

Flipping, he went facedown in the waves and stared into the darkness. It was like staring into the darkness of his lonely, hopeless future. He couldn't bear it.

On his back again, he considered returning to the krispin city a bit further up the coast. The idea of living amongst the party lifestyle and devil-may-care attitudes left a bad taste in his mouth. For now, at least, it was out of the question.

The storm intensified and thunder blasted the night, creating ripples in the waves for a second. Lightning zipped and zigzagged through the clouds, making an amazing show. Then the bolts came down. All around him, electricity struck the water with sizzling cracks.

Kyleal closed his eyes and waited. For a moment, he understood how Brandine had given up and waited for death. She had wanted freedom from her suffering. So did he.

Something soft brushed against his back a moment before it grabbed him by the throat and dragged him under.

Chapter Five

Brandine positioned herself above her angel and shoved him under. Instantly, her tail became two legs. It took everything in her to swim toward the bottom. She moved her hand from his throat and grasped him under the arms, planting her lips to his.

He tried to push her off, but she held tight. She would never have guessed she could swim so powerfully with legs instead of a tail, but she pulled strength and will from deep within. She had too much to lose. When his back hit the sand, she hugged him close and kissed him harder. He kissed her back, but she sensed his reluctance.

Releasing his mouth, she said, "You can't leave."

"You don't understand."

"I do." Why didn't he fight?

"No, you don't."

"Stop arguing with me." She kissed the tip of his nose. "I'm strong again, thanks to you. I'm yours, now. And you're mine."

He averted his gaze. "I'm not anybody's. I'm a krispin, remember?"

"I know what you are. I know *you*. You're part of me." It was liberating to say.

"Then you know I'll only betray you in time."

She needed to see his expression. "Let's go back to the cave. We can work this out."

He shoved her and used his webbed feet to gain some distance. "There is no 'working this out,' Brandine. I can't change what I am. I'm sorry I didn't listen to you. I'm sorry I bonded you to me."

She glared at him and used her tail to propel herself at him. Shoving with all her might, she said, "I'm not sorry. I'd do it again."

He blinked. "You would?"

"Yes. Could we please talk about this?"

He shook his head. "There's nothing to talk about. I'm setting you free."

She shoved him again, knocking him another twenty feet through the murky ocean. "You *can't* set me free, Kyleal. It's not your right."

"It's over, Brandine. Give it up."

"I'm not giving up anything." With anger increasing her strength, she grasped his steely arms and shoved. This time, she didn't let go. Employing her legs, she swam with all her might and worked her way along the rock ridge. "You're going to listen to me."

White teeth flashed in the shadowy depths. "I like you feisty."

"Good, because feisty is what I am." She swam harder.

"You're not going to change my mind." He tried to shake her off, but she held on tenaciously.

"Don't worry. I'm not going to try." She fought a smile.

"Then what's this about?"

She shook her head, needing her breath now to get them back to the cave before he realized she tired. He had tremendous strength and could overpower her and escape now that her reflexes began to wane.

The soft glow of his home lit a half-circle of sand beside the ridge. With the last of her energy, she executed a final burst and drove him down and inside. She threw her arms wide, blocking the exit and panting.

He swam at her in a threatening way but stopped short of touching her. "I could have easily evaded you out there. I *let* you bring me here."

"Good." She jutted her chin, suspecting he was right and wondering why he hadn't fought her more. "Then maybe you'll listen to me."

"You don't realize how bad I am for you. If you did, you wouldn't have brought me here." He swam a circuit around the cave then came to her with disappointment in his expression. "That was an impressive show of power, for a mermaid who was as weak as you when I carried you in here."

"You gave me the power when you saved my life. I'm whole. And I'm not going to lie down and let you swim away. Krispin or not, you're with me."

"And what happens when I decide to play unfaithful with the krispin population, again?" Disappointment turned to sadness, the corners of his mouth pulled firm.

She took a deep breath. Would he believe her? Would he listen? "You won't."

"I will. It's how I'm made, Brandine. Maybe not tomorrow or next week, but I will."

She went to him and placed a hand on his chest. "You won't," she whispered. "Trust me."

"How can I?" His agonizing struggle came through in his broken voice. His eyes never left hers. "I'm different but I'm not *that* different."

"You are. You're not just a krispin anymore." She held her breath, willing him to stay.

"Then what am I?"

"You're *my* krispin. Tell me you don't know me—my heart, my will, my desire."

He pressed his lips together and fingered a tendril of her hair. "I do." His eyes widened as if he realized this for the first time. "I don't understand it." His Adam's apple bobbed.

"Please don't be frightened. This is a good thing. Will you let me help you understand?"

He nodded, his hungry gaze devouring hers, seeking answers.

"I'm bonded to you, yes?"

"Yes."

Brandine wanted to kiss him, but he needed her words more at the moment. "The bonding that happened—you were there, too. Our essences combined for a brief time." She gently circled her palm on his chest, needing a physical connection with him. "The bonding was *ours*."

He glanced at her hand. "No, that's not possible. Krispins don't bond."

"With each other, no. But I'm not a krispin. Mermen can bond to mermaids. Humans can bond to mermaids—"

"Krispins," he said in a deep, breathy voice.

"Yes. Krispins can bond to mermaids"

Kyleal closed his eyes and remained perfectly still. "You're saying I'm bonded to you."

Resisting the urge to hug him, she waited. He had to accept it. If he didn't, she'd face a lifetime of chasing him.

"I've never heard of a krispin bonding to anyone." The sadness remained, but a light of hope blossomed within his pale gaze.

She placed her other hand next to the first. "Do you really need to hear of another? What's the truth in your heart? In your own krispin heart?" *Accept this. Love me.*

* * * *

Kyleal's skin was too small for his body, and he would come out of it in a second. The only thing holding him together was her touch. His brain threatened to explode. He tried his hardest to wrap his mind around the idea that he could be life-mated to the most beautiful creature he'd ever met. Could it be true? Dread warred with elation. If he hadn't bonded with her like she said, he would break her heart. If he had…If he had…

"Kyleal?" She blinked stunning purple eyes at him. "What do you want?"

"All I've ever wanted was a life worth living. A purpose." He'd never put it in words, but now that he did, he discovered how driving a force that desire had been all along.

"And now?"

Flea swam in and settled on the bed. The fluke blinked and waited, as if his answer mattered to the fish, too.

And now? He had saved her life—twice. He had accomplished something selfless. He'd acted outside his own interest. "And now, I've had a taste of adventure."

She shook her head. "What does that mean?"

"It means I don't want to stay here and stare at the ceiling for days at a time. There are things to be done. Places to go. I can make a difference." For a second, he couldn't catch his breath. His chest heaved as he drew water in gulps. "This is unprecedented."

Her arched brows came together above the bridge of her pert nose. "That you have work? You didn't have work before?"

Aghast, he stared at her. "No. Of course not. Krispins have no purpose above meeting their physical needs—eating, sleeping, mating. There's fun in hunting and mating, but nothing to accomplish beyond the moment of the experience. Have you?"

Her sweet lips curled at the corners. "Well, yes. Every mermaid has work. We do much in the ocean—helping whale migrations, hunting with dolphins, herding sardines through the Sargasso, advancing phytoplankton blooms. There's so much to do. We travel a lot, see wonderful sea creatures…"

His head spun. Oh, to do such things. See such things. "What else?"

She beamed. "We get to meet turtle hatchlings as they leave the beach and enter the ocean for the first time. It's hard work fighting the large fish that come to feed on them, but it's so rewarding. We show them beds of vegetation to hide in and help them find their first meals. They're so cute."

In the corner of his vision, Flea blinked from the bed then fluttered to the entrance. There in the sand, a pretty pink-tinged fluke waited. Flea settled beside it, blinked a farewell then swam away with the other. He took her hands with his, but left them on his chest. "Brandine."

Chapter Six

"I feel it." He moved her hands above his heart, his eyes filled with tender affection. "I didn't think it was possible."

"A life of purpose?" She searched his face eagerly. Would he love her? Could he?

"A life of purpose with the one I love at my side. I bonded with you but didn't know what had happened. I thought something had gone wrong. That God was punishing me with torturous feelings because I'd done something against His will. I didn't know what I felt was love. Love for you. Love for a lifetime."

She gasped, her mouth falling agape. "You love me? Wait, you believe in God? The one God?"

"Yes. The one God who isn't punishing me. He's rewarding me. I don't know what I've done to deserve you, but He sent you to me. On a wild, magical current of His making, he whisked you to me from a hundred miles away and gave me the task of saving your life. I don't think I would have believed I was capable until you showed up and I didn't have a choice."

"Didn't you?" She grinned. He loved her.

"No. Any other krispin would have abandoned you the moment you became less than entertaining. But I'm different. There's something in me that needs a higher mission. There's something in me that needs you. Brandine, my love, will you stay with me forever? Be my life-mate?" He stiffened like he expected her to deny him.

Euphoria lifted her as though she had wings instead of him. "There's nothing else I want. Come with me, Kyleal. There is so much to do. Saving baby whales from giant squid, rescuing young tuna that lose their course on runs—"

"Helping humans from sinking ships out to sea…" He oozed impatient anticipation.

"Exactly. There's always work to do, fun to be had, and adventures to experience. Are you ready?" She looked forward to sharing her life with him. He'd bring newness and excitement to each event.

"Yes." Lowering his mouth to hers, he breathed deeply through his nostrils, the movement of water caressing her cheek. He ended the sweet kiss and gazed at her with an intensity that made her stomach quiver. "But first, there's something we've got to do."

"What?"

He raked fingers through her hair, brushing it away from her ear then removed her halter with one hand. "This." He hugged her close and moved to the bed.

Heavy expectation formed low in her belly. Between her legs, a throbbing began. Kyleal lay on the bed and brought her atop him. She straddled him, liking the versatility of legs. Under his pelvic fin, he hardened against her. Her blood ran hot through her veins at the knowledge that she affected him this way. Moisture spilled from her, coating her folds.

He took her by the hips and lifted her. Reaching with one hand, he shifted his pelvic fin aside and lowered her to his shaft. He didn't enter her, however.

"Foreplay," he said with a grin.

"We don't have to." She looked forward to having him inside her.

"Last time, it was a matter of life and death. Now, we do this for fun. Foreplay."

She smiled. "Okay. Foreplay." She took his nipples between thumbs and forefingers and plucked.

He gasped and returned the favor.

She gasped and laughed. "Sea-angel."

"Fish-woman."

Throwing back her head, she released her joy on a hearty guffaw.

He cupped her breasts, making them swell into his skimming fingers. He grazed her hard nipples with the pads of his thumbs. As electric pleasure bolted straight to her core, her juices flowed faster.

Her heartbeat quickened, as did her breathing. Hooking fingers behind her neck, he pulled her to him. His warm skin titillated her. It was exactly where she wanted to be for all time. Against him. Part of him.

He brought his lips to hers and they met in an open-mouthed kiss, tongues at the ready to enter into an erotic dance. When she tasted him, she had a sense that she'd come home. She'd never be alone again.

Closing her eyes, she drowned in him—his touch, his smell, his taste. Everything about him made her melt with wanting. Sending her hands over him, she took her time and learned every line, every texture of him. She marveled at his hard planes and deep dips compared with her rounded softness.

His shaft nudged her folds, making her anxious to be one with him. Reaching between them, she gripped his length.

"Brandine," he said on a moan. "I love you."

"I love you, Kyleal."

She fitted his tip to her entrance and rocked back to take him into her. Seating him completely, she delighted at the fullness he created in her. Every inch of him stretched her pulsing passage. Going upright, she gazed down on his handsome face. He was her sea-angel. Hers and only hers. The krispin was the most stunning male to behold, and she was privileged to be his life-mate.

"You have a good heart," she said, pressing a palm to his chest. Her ribs expanded with love for him.

His eyelids drooped, giving his eyes a sensual quality. Her body gripped his. Rocking her hips, she started a rhythm that built a heavenly pressure inside her womb. She sighed, enjoying his increased need, revealed by the thinning of his lips and the pull of skin over his cheekbones.

He took her shoulder and urged her low. Possessing her mouth in a passionate kiss, he levitated off the bed and flipping them using his powerful dorsal fin. With her legs still around his waist, he went to his knees and reset the pace.

Faster, steadier, he stroked into her. He planted hands on either side of her shoulders, his face poised above hers with an expression of intense concentration.

As the pleasure increased in leaping increments, Brandine closed her eyes and allowed him to sweep her away. Higher she climbed, propelled by his pounding thrusts. Their hips undulated. Their exhaled water mingled.

Before she could reach the pinnacle of release, however, he slowed. Each stroke filled her. She felt every inch of him.

"Kyleal," she begged. "Please."

"I love it when my feisty mermaid pleads so prettily." He offered her a pained smile.

His feisty mermaid. She adored the sound of it. Sending her fingers into his hair, she drew him into a kiss. She poured all her love into it and drank in his hunger for her.

The pressure began to build anew, this time faster and harder. Keeping pace, she met him thrust for thrust. Their panting matched. Their hearts beat as one.

He stroked quicker, each one letting his tip kiss her womb before he pulled nearly out of her then repeated the move. She gasped with each joining of their hips. Nearly to release, she strained for the last push that would take her over the edge.

"I need you. Now. Now," she cried.

"Aa-aa-aa!" Arching, he slammed into her, giving her the final shove she needed.

"Yes!" they yelled together.

Brandine arched as her being was yanked from her body. She rocketed into celestial heights with Kyleal holding onto her. They reached the point of weightlessness then exploded into each other. They rained to earth, their souls entwined in twinkling beauty, like falling stardust. As they hit the ocean, they separated and dove at top speed back into their bodies.

She gasped, arching. "Amazing," she breathed.

"Spectacular. Making love with you is like nothing else in this world. It's magical."

Magical. Yes. "I love you, Kyleal. My angel."

"I love you, Brandine. My everything."

The End

A Prince's Tail
By Sara Murphy

After being cheated on by her fiancée, Maggie returns to her cottage by the sea to batten down the hatches and mend her broken heart. Hearing the call from his mate, Tarman braves the wrath of his royal parents and the fury of a hurricane to find her. When Maggie finds the injured Tarman in her boat house she tends his wounds and he heals her heart.

* * *

I would like to thank: Laura Kitchell for pestering me until I started writing again and her continuing relentless support. The rest of Chesapeake Romance Writers for their encouragement. My family for their endless love and willingness to share me with my new passion.
And my husband who is my hero.

* * *

You can contact Sara through her website
www.sarakmurphy.com.

A Prince's Tail
By Sara Murphy

Chapter One

"I'm not running away from my problems," Maggie said into her cell phone headset as she wrestled trash cans into the storage area under her porch.

"You ran away from your wedding." Her mother's shrill voice made Maggie want to remove the headset. It wasn't the first time.

Instead, she latched shut the storage area door and said, "I caught him cheating on me with Angela. In the coat room. At our rehearsal dinner."

"Yes, but didn't he apologize?" Her mother believed that any man was better than no man at all.

Maggie pinched the bridge of her nose. "Sorry doesn't count when you say it with your pants down." She kicked a small statue of a fish. The little figure rolled down the slope to the brush that lined the beach front. Sighing, she trudged to retrieve it.

"Honey, I don't like the idea of you staying in that shack of yours with a hurricane coming in." Her mother was running out of options so she'd pulled out the safety card.

"Mom, it's more than a shack. I've lived here for years. My studio is here." Having given up too much of herself during her time with her ex-fiancée, Maggie was glad to return to her passion.

"Don't get me started on your *career*."

"Fine. I won't." Maggie picked up several more lawn ornaments and placed them in a cart. "So how's Dad?" Her mother couldn't pass up a chance to complain about her father.

"Oh, instead of canceling the caterer, he decided to cut the order and have it delivered to the house. He said it was to keep me from having to cook. Just looking out for me." She scoffed. "He just wanted an excuse to not follow his diet."

Since the diet was imposed by his wife and not a doctor, Maggie didn't worry over her father's antics. "Did he have anything to say about what Steve did?" Maggie asked, not sure if she wanted the answer.

"He sent the bill for the deposits on the band and the hall to Steve along with a warning to stay away from you. Honey, your Dad would forgive Steve if you did."

"Why do you want me to marry Steve so much?"

"You could use the security. The financial security."

Maggie looked over her empty yard then at the horizon filled with clouds. Her mother just wanted the best for her. Too bad hers was the way of the nineteen-fifties—marry well and act happy. But they'd gone around about their differing approaches to marriage before.

"I love you, Mom."

"I love you too, dear."

"I need to finish boarding up the windows."

"Fine, fine. I'll let you go. But what should I say to Steve if he asks about you?"

"Tell him I'm glad he cheated before we got married rather than after, saved me the hassle of a divorce."

After hanging up with her mother, Maggie turned to her home. Her little cottage at the entrance to the inlet wasn't much. Certainly not something her mother would see as worthy of being called a summer house. For Maggie, it was a perfect fit. The siding resembled dark wood shingle and stood out against the bright grasses and sand dunes behind the house. Situated at the end of the beach and set back from the road a bit, most times she could imagine she had the entire beach to herself. In the off-season, it was true.

However, this wasn't the off season. It smelled as though the family renting the house south of hers was cooking out.

Tempted to ignore their stupidity, she almost went into the house. Then with a sigh, she walked to the sand and along the beach until she spotted their deck. Sure enough, toys and chairs remained strewn about the yard. The mother and father kissed passionately at the grill while three children aged between thirteen and eight ran past her to and from the water.

"Hello," Maggie called to the parents.

The couple jolted apart and the woman started toward her, shooting a grin over her shoulder at her husband. "Hello, are you our neighbor? Sorry we didn't come by and introduce ourselves, but we've been busy."

"Sure. I understand." Maggie dodged another running child. "Well, I don't know if you have television here, but there's a hurricane headed this way."

"Oh yeah, we know all about that." The woman waved her hand as if dismissing the storm.

"We'll start getting rain in a couple hours. The tides are treacherous already so you might want to call in your children."

"They're barely in the water."

"I've seen a tide pull a grown man off his feet." She decided not to share that the man was very drunk at the time.

"Allen said that these houses are meant to withstand a hurricane. And this is just a category one. We don't have to evacuate."

"I'm not saying that." Maggie managed the kindest smile she could muster. Tourists bought her artwork after all. "Just, in the interest of safety, get the kids out of the water, pick up the debris that the wind could blow around, and board up the house."

The woman's eyes got wide. "Are you saying we need to go to the hardware store?"

The Millers, the owners of the house, kept boards in a shed. She led the way and showed the husband what to do for the windows. One thing she could say about all those children, when they got started at a job, things went fast. With the neighbors situated, she returned to her preparations. As the rain started to fall, she'd managed to get the rest of her boards on her own windows. She walked to the inlet side of her property to check the little boat house.

Built out of Locust trees over the water, the boathouse would probably last longer than the cottage. The canoe she sometimes took up the inlet hung on the wall. The little boat house had a dock for a floor on one side and an opening that allowed her to row out at the far end. This let her go rowing without hauling the canoe down to a beach. Good thing, because on the inlet side, she didn't have a beach—more of a marshy drop-off.

Satisfied everything was in order, she hurried into the cottage. Selecting a book, she settled in to enjoy the storm. Maggie loved being cozy in a house while a storm raged outside. The only thing missing was a man to share the experience. Ah well, no man meant no one to fight with either.

* * * *

A voice made Tarman turn on his tail. His little sister, eight-year-old Annalie, swam up to him. Of all his siblings, she was his favorite. They understood each other so well, and she seemed to sense when he needed to talk. Today, however, he wasn't in the mood for company.

"Where are you going?" Annalie's little voice cracked a bit in her effort to catch up to him.

"Anna, I can't marry the maid from the north."

"But Mama wants you too. She said it's important, like Marcan's wedding."

"Marcan is the eldest, and someday he'll be king. His marriage was for the realm." It also didn't hurt that Marcan already loved the maid he was called to marry two weeks prior.

"You don't love her." Anna tilted her head, considering him. "I don't think she wants to love you either, you know. She keeps talking about a lobster farmer back home. Maybe if you explained to Mama, she would let you marry someone else."

"I've talked to Mother." He crouched to her level and looked her in the eye. "Anna, I need to mate, but the northern maid isn't for me. Do you understand?"

Her little head nodded. "When you find her, can I meet her?"

"I'll let everyone meet her."

"Promise?" She pouted, and her chin quivered.

"I promise." Tarman hugged his little sister. "We will come back to visit." He glanced over her shoulder at the flurry of activity near the entrance to the palace. Had they already started looking for him?

"Don't tell anyone which way I went, alright?" And after giving his sister one last hug, he shooed her toward the castle then turned and swam to freedom.

He trusted her not to tell anyone. And when he did get settled, he would bring his mate to meet Anna. He had to. He'd never broken a promise to her. The palace sat away from the rest of the city, which made leaving unnoticed rather easy. No one appeared to notice when he swam past the boundary.

The open water flowed around him, refreshing, liberating. Reaching out with his feelings, he determined the direction of his true mate. West. Without hesitation, Tarman headed west. A man was meant to find his mate. His parents knew that as much as anyone. When he came of age and hadn't been called to a maid, they panicked and chose a wife for him.

Many men didn't sense the call until they were several years older than he. The farther the maid, the harder it was to hear her call. But a week ago, Tarman heard her. Instead of hearing her in a steady call, he only heard his maid intermittently. This anomaly made him afraid to tell anyone. It amounted to having an imaginary courtship in the next town. No one would believe him.

So he set off to find his love, the one that would complete him.

* * * *

Finding her is harder than I expected, he thought as the current tossed him around. In his eagerness, he swam directly into a hurricane.

The call had gone silent, or perhaps been deafened by crashing waves and howling wind. Buffeted and rolled several times, he tried to dive and evade the chaos of the surface only to be cut off by a pod of dolphins. He shot to the surface, expecting to break the surface of the dark water. Instead, he slammed into something hard.

Falling back, Tarman tried to clear his head. He tasted gasoline. He must have struck a human vessel. Shaking fog from his vision, he flicked his tail to propel toward the faint trace of the maid he desired.

The movement caused a searing pain to course through his body. He curled to see what had struck him but couldn't see past a cloud of blood. Steeling himself against the pain, he pushed forward. Now, he not only struggled against the currents of the storm but against his failing strength.

After what seemed like hours, he found himself thrown against a wooden post. The current pressed and would have moved him past it but he grabbed and held on. Above him, a dock loomed. The surface of the water seemed calmer here. A structure of some kind sheltered the water.

Holding the post with one hand, he reached out with the other and gripped the side of the dock. His shoulder almost wrenched out of its socket as the current hooked his tail and tried to take him.

After managing to grip the dock with both hands, he paused and took a deep breath and, with a thrust of his tail, pushed out of the water. Landing hard on the wood of the dock, he gasped for breath. A second later, he realized out of the water, anyone could happen upon him. He couldn't stay in mer-form. Fighting pain and fatigue, he focused and changed into a human. In the safety of his meager shelter, he lost consciousness.

Chapter Two

Maggie paced the length of her galley kitchen. She could see some damage through the small window beside her back door. Some of the siding had come loose as always, and the neighbors had missed a few things in their clean-up. Now their grill rolled across her lawn.

She wanted to leave the house and clean up the debris. Any minute she expected the storm's eye to pass over.

When the banging of the loose siding stopped, she opened the door and walked out into the eerie quiet. The sun shined and humidity weighted the air. She gasped, the oppressive air hard to breathe. She wouldn't have much time in the eye of the storm. Perhaps half an hour, only time enough to gather the big stuff. Like the grill.

Bits of siding and several toys from the neighbor's yard lay strewn about. She grabbed the handle of a big wheel and dragged it to the storage area under her porch. With all the other things already stored inside, nothing else would fit. Perhaps she could stuff the grill and toys in the boathouse to keep them from causing damage when the second half of the storm hit.

Taking the handle of the grill in her other hand, and several of the siding pieces, she dragged them around the side of the house and down the slight slope. The ground squished the closer she got to the boathouse. Releasing the grill and dropping the big wheel, she moved to open the lock.

Over the sound of waves slamming onto the shore, she could hear moaning from inside the boathouse.

Immediately concerned, she managed to get the lock open in record time and threw the door wide.

A man lay prone on the dock. For a second it seemed as though he had a tail. She moved inside and to the left, allowing more light to enter.

The groaning form on her dock appeared to be part man, part fish. She'd sculpted enough merpeople to know what lay before her, though she still couldn't believe it.

The merman groaned again, and his tail flopped. Slits on his neck appeared and gapped open then disappeared as his mouth gasped. His whole body shuddered. He couldn't breathe.

With the fact that she had no idea how to help him screaming in her mind, she rushed to his side anyway. As she knelt, she noticed an injury on his tail. Another shudder changed his tail to legs. Muscular, human looking, yet his right leg still had a deep gash on the inside. Tugging off her blouse, she wrapped it around his thigh.

Convinced the makeshift bandage was tight enough, she allowed her gaze to roam his body. Oh yes, he was definitely male. Her breath caught, and her mouth went dry. Though the air sweltered, she shivered in her tank top. She should get him into the house before the storm started again, but she couldn't help wondering where he kept *it* when he had a tail.

"I'm up here." The deep voice startled her, and she quickly shifted her gaze to his face.

"Um, sorry. Um…" God, she was staring at him. She had been staring at him, at his…Oh, God. "A storm's coming. You should come inside."

"I should." But he didn't move, and when he stared at her, he seemed to look inside her.

His penetrating gaze made her warmer than what had captured her attention merely seconds before.

"Can you stand?" He nodded and she reached to help him. "Do you know how to walk?" He said nothing. Was she being rude? She should just shut up. Though he wobbled a bit, he walked fine considering her shirt tied around his thigh.

How a merman knew how to walk, she had no idea. Perhaps this wasn't his first time on land, or maybe he had taken classes on how to act human. She choked on a laugh as she secured the door to the boat house.

She accompanied him across the yard as he slowly made his way up the slope. The wind carried the sound of laughing children. She sincerely hoped the neighbors' kids didn't run along her beach. How would she explain the amazingly naked man she supported?

She opened the door and allowed him to enter. Just then the eldest of the neighbor children came running to her house.

"Mom wanted me to ask if you wanted to come to our post hurricane party. Dad said he's going to fire up the grill again." The boy was about thirteen and couldn't take his eyes from her cleavage.

Maggie sighed. "I just had to stow your grill in my boathouse. You need to tell your parents that the hurricane isn't over and the second half will be along in a minute."

The boy tore his gaze away from her chest and regarded her with suspicion. "Dad said it was over."

People really need to get their facts straight before they pass them on to their children. "Do you see that?" she asked, pointing over his shoulder toward the dark and ominous wall of clouds. "That's the wall of the eye. It has the strongest winds of the storm. Tell your family to get back inside the house."

She turned and entered her cottage without waiting to see the boy's reaction. The merman stood in the doorway to the living room. After raking him with her gaze—*damn you look good*—she motioned him to follow her into the bathroom.

She wanted to babble, to distract herself from his amazing physique, his proximity, and the scent of his skin. From everything that made her want to turn around and throw herself at him.

With her lips firmly pressed together she, motioned him to sit on the toilet lid, then pulled out her first aid kit.

Unwrapping her blouse from his thigh, she knelt in front of him. It seemed the salt water had done some of the cleaning and sterilizing for her.

Still, she dabbed a bit of peroxide on the wound and tried to ignore the proof of his gender so close to her hand.

"You *are* beautiful," he said, his strange accent adding an allure to words she'd never believed until he spoke them. She stared into his eyes and thought he looked strangely familiar.

"Thank you," she said. *You amazingly sexy, naked merman you.* She leaned to shelves across from the sink, picked up a hand towel, and laid it on his lap. "Uh…"

He tilted his head to the side.

"Um. When I'm done here, I'll get you some clothes."

"It was very nice of you to warn that child."

Why did he insist on complementing her? Whenever Steve had, it made her think she didn't deserve it. The man in front of her didn't have that snide tone Steve always used. Perhaps he really meant the things he said.

"They're tourists. They have no idea of the dangers of a hurricane. It looks like you got caught in the storm yourself." She placed ointment and a bandage on his wound.

"I focused on your call and didn't pay attention to where I was headed."

"Um, okay." She didn't want to let on she didn't understand what he meant.

Fingers reached out to stroke her cheek. "I have been drawn to you."

She stood and backed away. She should be offended or outraged, but instead all she could muster was confusion. "Y-y-you don't even know my name," she stammered.

He stood without a wince, towel falling to the floor with a whisper, and cupped her chin. "I've traveled here to meet you. We were meant to be together. I have never known a deeper truth in my life."

"I…" She was lost. What could she say to such a declaration? In a bar, she would laugh and find a security guard, but here in her house with a man who not fifteen minutes ago had a tail… She believed him. "How is that possible?"

"My people know who they are meant to be with. We are drawn to our mate. As I was drawn to you." His arms slipped around her waist. One hand stayed at the small of her back and the other pressed between her shoulder blades. His lips lowered to hers slowly. She had plenty of time to avoid them, but something in her ached for them.

His lips were soft yet firm and felt as though they controlled all the muscles in the small of her back. These muscles tightened and tingled, spreading wonderful tremors throughout her body.

Her mind swam, tossed in the chaos of what she wanted to do and what she should do. All her life, she'd done what she should do. Sensible. Practical. Now she wanted to follow the orders her body screamed.

Unable to make sense of it all, she stepped back from him and bumped into the shelving.

He dropped his arms to his sides, the corner of his mouth quirked into a half smile. "My name is Tarman."

"Um, I'm Maggie." He was so close, so manly and oh, so naked. She licked suddenly dry lips. "I need a drink. Do you want a drink?" Her gaze wandered downward. "Um, clothes. You need clothes first."

"Whatever you wish."

"Clothes." She hung onto the word to try and focus her thoughts as she went to her bedroom. "Steve only came to the cottage once, but he left one of his bags when he stormed out. I should have realized Steve wasn't for me when he brought two suitcases and a duffel bag full of clothes for a weekend."

Again with the babbling. She crushed her lips into a thin line and managed to restrain herself from mentioning that Steve only tolerated her quaint hovel for two hours. So many signs she should have seen.

"Here," she said, pulling out a pair of sweat pants and a tee-shirt. She held them to him. When he took them, his fingers brushed hers and an energy passed between them.

Instead of jerking away at the shock, Tarman clasped his other hand over hers. "Thank you," he said, staring directly into her eyes and making her feel as though he could see her thoughts.

After another beat, he looked away and moved to slip on the clothes. Having his body hidden should have made her calmer, but she couldn't help picturing him without them. The idea of his muscular arms wrapped around her, pulling her close to his hard body…

What was she doing? How could she be so attracted to him? Before her stood a merman. A strong, sexy, um… Closing her eyes, she tried to regain her composure. But they flew open again when he cleared his throat.

"You mentioned a drink," he said.

"Sure." She wanted to move away. She lifted her foot, but stepped toward him instead. A fog fell over her, as if she'd had several glasses of wine, and for a moment, just a moment, she allowed impulse to control her.

She placed her palm on his stomach, feeling the hard muscles through the cotton of the shirt. As her hand reached his well-toned chest, she gripped the fabric and pulled him to her. She longed for his mouth on hers and couldn't stand being without it for another second.

A little voice at the back of her mind wondered where this was coming from, but the rest of her didn't care. It had been years since she'd felt passion like this, and she wanted it to flourish.

Pressing her body against his, she could have leapt for joy when his hand caressed her back and pulled her hips closer to his. Suddenly they were off balance and falling. They landed on the foot of her bed.

Tarman's long wavy hair framed his face as he smiled up at her. They were in bed. The fog lifted as if she'd been hit with a bucket of cold water. Placing her hands on either side of his body, she pushed off of him.

"I'm sorry," she muttered. What had she been thinking? It wasn't like her to just jump into bed. "Let me get you that drink." She strode to the kitchen without looking back.

She filled a couple glasses with ice and poured lemonade. A nice cooling drink. She felt so flushed and overheated. What had gotten into her?

He came into the kitchen while she held the pitcher to her forehead.

"Take one." She waved a hand and returned the pitcher to the refrigerator.

"Thank you," he said and took a sip. "Ah, lemonade. I haven't had this in years."

That surprised her. "You've had lemonade before?"

"This isn't the first time I've been on land."

She was about to ask about his previous visit when a slam at the front of the house stopped her. The entire structure rattled then several faint popping sounds sent her into action.

"Crap." Glass in hand, she raced for her studio.

Chapter Three

She loved her studio. A sitting room at one time, it had three windows and provided an inspiring view of both the inlet and the ocean from the corner of the cottage. In preparation for the storm, she'd boarded the windows, so she was sure one of them hadn't broken.

Her kiln stood in a corner away from the windows where her work table waited. Lining the walls, shelves held sculptures. Some wanted painting while others dried before firing. She sold most of her finished work in shops by the public beach, but some of the figures she just loved and couldn't part with. These had a shelf all their own.

One set in particular she'd dreamt. The first night back in the house, she dreamt of a gathering of merpeople circling around a couple. The two in the center had what looked like ribbons wrapped around their tails, holding them together. For the past two weeks, she'd sculpted the wedding party, starting with the apparent bride and groom.

Though not broken, they had toppled and knocked several pots she'd thrown as presents for her future in-laws to the floor.

She chuckled at the shattered pottery. If this wasn't a sign not to forgive Steve, she didn't know what was. She reached for a broom and dustpan in the corner behind the door.

"Something large must have slammed into the house," she said as she swept the broken pottery into a dustpan. "Watch your feet in here. This stuff can cut you."

"I'd like to help." He stepped around broken bits and reached to right the toppled newlyweds. "Where did you get this?" he asked, holding the statue in his hand.

Maggie stood, dumping the dustpan into a garbage can. "I had a dream about them a couple weeks or so ago. It seemed like a wedding." She wasn't sure what to make of his expression. "I'm sculpting everyone that I saw." She pointed at the other statues that lined the shelf.

Tarman reached for another and laughed.

"What?" His laugh was so full of delight she couldn't help but smile as well. "What is it?"

"Me."

"I'm sorry?"

"You've sculpted my brother's wedding. "This," he said, holding out the couple statue to her, "is my brother and his bride." He pointed to another. "The Popa, the man who performed the ceremony." Then he pointed to several in succession. "My mother, my father, my little sister, Anna."

He turned and caressed Maggie's cheek with the back of one finger. "And this, my love, is me." He indicated the last statue on the shelf.

The miniature stood only six inches tall, but it had his face. She remembered carving it. She'd closed her eyes after completing his face and wished for someone so loving as he seemed.

She set the statue she held on its place on the shelf and reached out to the statue of Tarman. Her finger rubbed over the statue's chest and down the tail then she looked up at the man himself. "How is this possible?"

Tarman took her hand and led her to the futon by the door. "I told this to you before. We are meant to be together. That's why you dreamt of my brother's wedding. We are connected, you and I." He traced a fingertip along her jaw, and she closed her eyes and leaned into his touch.

"I wished for you that day, too." His warm breath pulsed against her lips as he spoke. And like the tide to a sandcastle, the last of her reservations were washed away.

He kissed her. His lips parted and his tongue slowly traced the seam of her lips. She allowed him entrance. She tasted him in turn and recognized the citrus of the lemonade.

Deepening the kiss, she struggled to hide a moan. She loved the taste of him. Adored the way his hands held her in an embrace that made her feel protected. Loved in a way no man had ever made her experience love. She ran fingers into his silken shoulder-length hair, and then cupped the back of his neck.

He responded by running a hand under her bottom and scooping her into his arms.

Startled, she let out a weak shriek. "What are you doing?"

"Your studio is hardly the appropriate place to make love for the first time." He carried her through the house and into her bedroom.

Her heart leapt. That he thought of it as making love made her want to do it all the more. As he entered her bedroom, she nuzzled his neck. He gently laid her on the bed and stretched out beside her.

She kept her eyes on his as he traced his fingertips from her neck down her chest, over the cloth of her tank top and between her breasts to her belly button. Every nerve followed the path of those fingers. By the time they reached their destination, nothing else existed but his caress. Not the storm that raged outside. Not the bed beneath her.

When he reached the waist band of her shorts, he slipped a finger under, hooked it and pulled. Her breath caught in her throat and his brow furrowed.

"This shouldn't hurt you," he said.

"No." She smiled. "I can't wait for you to touch me."

His grin was radiant. "Oh, in that case." He ran his hands up her sides, catching the fabric and pulling her shirt over her head. Retracing their path along her body, his fingers seemed to send out electric sparks. This time when he found the waistband of her shorts, he pulled them off.

She expected him to return to kiss her, to lie beside her and work his magic on all the parts of her that ached for it. Instead, she felt pressure on her feet. He'd gripped her foot and squeezed, the tips of his fingers pressing into the arch of her foot.

Had she ever had someone rub her feet before? Couldn't have. If she had, she would have remembered. Oh, wow it felt so good. She closed her eyes and sighed.

Just when every muscle in her body relaxed, he left her feet. His amazingly talented hands massaged her calves then tickled the back of her knees as they traveled to her thighs. She spread her legs in anticipation of what would come next.

He must touch her. She needed him to, but he moved past what any man would have eagerly focused on and leaned to kiss her abdomen. The sweatpants he wore rubbed against her thigh, reminding her he was still dressed.

"I think you can take those clothes off now," she said, reaching for his shirt.

"All in good time." He chuckled and kissed the valley between her breasts. A line of kisses led him to her neck. His tee shirt brushed against her nipples. Her body longed for him, moistening the part of her he'd so casually ignored.

He lightly licked her earlobe. She couldn't stand it and reached for him, sliding her hands across his hard body. Tracing every line of muscle with the tips of her fingers made her hotter.

Finally, he made his way back to her lips and kissed her softly and deeply. His arms encircled her, pressing his body to hers. When he pulled back, she opened her eyes and found his gaze only inches from hers. Silently she begged for him to appease the parts of her that ached for his touch.

He stood and undressed. Again she marveled at his body, so toned and defined she couldn't wait to have it against her. Her gaze landed on what had enraptured her the first time she saw him. Just the sight of it fulfilling its potential made her mouth water.

She shifted to get a good angle and kissed it, slowly opening her mouth and flicking her tongue over him. His gasp made her smile. His turn to go a little crazy. Keeping her pace slow, she explored him until his knees seemed to go weak and he leaned against the bed.

"Did you like that?" she asked.

"Oh yes," he replied, breathless. "But not as much as you'll like this." He laid a hand on her shoulder, pushing her onto the bed and kneeling over her. Again, he kissed her mouth, but this time when he moved away, he cupped her breasts. After running his thumb over their peaks, he took them one at a time into his mouth. Teeth and tongue eased the ache and brought her to panting.

He lifted his head. "Did you like it?" His voice had deepened into a husky baritone that rumbled like thunder.

"Yes," she breathed.

"And this?" He ran a hand up the inside of her thigh and explored her, causing her body to arch with release.

She opened her eyes and could see her need echoed in his expression. "Tarman," she whispered. He could have continued to drive her crazy with desire. They both knew it. Instead, he slowly entered her.

In that instant, something clicked. She became one with him. She felt the curve of her own body beneath him. How the pressure of her walls around his length sent rays of extreme pleasure through his body. His pleasure was hers.

Returning to herself, she realized he'd paused. It had happened to him, too. They had meshed—body and mind.

"My love," he said then kissed her deeply.

The part of her that wanted to stop, to analyze what had happened, gave way immediately to the all-encompassing rhythm that beat throughout her body.

She gave over to it and, in doing so, to him. She allowed herself to be swept away on a tide of pleasure.

* * * *

When the storm of their love-making subsided and they lay in each other's arms, Maggie breathed in the scent of him and sighed. "I don't ever want to move."

"Me either," he said, running a hand up and down a small patch of skin on her upper arm.

"Something more happened just now, while we…"

"We've bonded," he said. He caught her look and laughed. I've never done it before, but they tell us what to expect.

"Bonded." The idea should have terrified her. After all, she'd only just avoided marrying a man who would have treated her like dirt. Instead, she liked the idea of it. "It's like being married?"

"We are now joined forever. There is a ceremony, but that's technically not necessary."

"Will I have to live in the ocean with you?" Maggie asked, reaching out to run a finger across his jaw.

Chuckling, he kissed her palm. "Could you? Do you have that gift? I understood that humans can't shift forms."

"I can't, that I know of." His smile warmed her like sunbathing never had.

Chapter Four

Tarman held Maggie beside him. She was human, but everything he'd always wanted. It wasn't just looks, though she was absolutely stunning. Her brown hair and eyes were exotic and tantalizing, but her attitude toward life seemed so close to his. Her soul had called to his. Her soft skin smelled like the scent of the flowers on her dresser. The bright plants, flowers, lilacs, smelled intoxicating. So did Maggie. Now that they had bonded, nothing could force them apart except perhaps his parents. They had plans for his future that he had effectively ruined. If he returned to the ocean, they could force him to return permanently. More than anything, Tarman wanted to stay with Maggie. Nothing else mattered. Not the nation his family ruled and certainly not the marriage arranged for him.

But he'd promised Anna could meet his mate. If he went back…if he went back to the ocean, to his home, there would be no escaping his parents or their wrath. He could let them think he was killed in the storm. That's what they would most likely think anyway. But that would break Anna's heart.

The beautiful woman stirring in his arms interrupted his train of thought.

"You're going to go back to the sea, aren't you?" She wrapped his arm tighter around her waist.

"No, I intend to stay with you." He brushed hair from her face.

"But you will return to tell your family what's happened?" Her lovely face turned to him, eyes wide. "They should know what's happened to you. That you're safe."

"You are right, of course." It pleased him that she thought of his family. "You should know that if I were to return, there would be very little chance I would be able to come back."

"What do you mean?"

He shifted onto his elbow and gazed down on her brilliantly bewildered features. "My parents would have me marry a maid from the Northern Sea. I would not be free to return. I was able to leave before because I escaped without their knowing. If I returned now, they would make sure I had no other opportunity."

"So you snuck out of the house without telling your family, your kingdom, where you were going?"

He considered her. "My family rules the east sea." He brushed another strand of hair from her face. "I've never taken a mate, and until recently, I've never heard the call. So my family arranged a marriage for me. I left before they could coerce me into joining without love."

"Why didn't you tell them you heard a call from me?"

"They wouldn't have believed me, or even if they did, they wouldn't have accepted it. To my knowledge, no merman has ever been called to a land woman."

"I think you're wonderful."

He could hear the *but* coming and cringed.

"But you have responsibility to your family."

He held a finger to her lips. "I have set aside that obligation."

"They don't know you have. For all they know, you ran off to play with the whales."

The idea of playing with the impassive creatures made him chuckle.

"What?"

"One doesn't play with whales."

She rolled her eyes. "Be that as it may, they have no idea what happened to you. They could be searching for you right now."

His thoughts hadn't extended that far. If they started a search, wouldn't Anna say something to stop it? Sometimes his little sister could be very literal. She might allow search parties to go out in order to keep her promise to him.

After a few moments, Maggie rubbed his arm. "Will they be able to get the treaty any other way? There won't be war because you left?"

Tarman laughed. "No, there hasn't been a war in over three hundred years. The treaty was more a formality because they wanted me to get married than for any other purpose."

Again, she seemed to consider his words. What a wonder it was to have someone actually listen. "Well then." She rolled and sat on his abdomen. "I think it would be in the best interest of your people for your highness to stay here and insure your people continue to have good relations with the land dwellers."

"I defer to your wisdom, my love." He'd have to figure out a way to keep his promise to his sister without returning to the sea.

Maggie tilted her head. "I don't hear the wind anymore. I think the storm may have passed."

"Did you want to start cleaning up?"

The corner of her mouth quirked in that endearing way it did. "I'd like that." Getting out of bed, Tarman couldn't help glancing at her lovely curves as she gathered her clothes. A quick glance over her shoulder and he was caught, but her smile warmed him. They would have the rest of their lives to tumble back into bed. He pulled on his clothes.

"We'll need to go shopping too." She tugged at his tee-shirt. "You can't wear this forever and I don't know if any of Steve's other clothes will fit."

"Whenever you want to go," he said, running his hand through her hair.

"You know, most men hate shopping." She laughed.

"Yes well, I'm not a man now am I?"

She giggled. "After we clean up, we'll head out." She opened a cabinet and removed some plastic bags. As she bent, her bottom faced him and he enjoyed the view. She led the way to the yard. Following her, he marveled at how extraordinarily happy she made him. As he took a bag from her, he pressed his lips to hers, and silently vowed his love to her forever.

Chapter Five

Maggie was acutely aware of the man cleaning debris beside her. He wanted to stay. Excitement welled inside her. What they'd shared wasn't just sex. It wasn't simply a matter of physically enjoying each other.

"Are you sure this isn't bothering your leg?" she asked, holding her breath for an answer.

"I am not bothered by it." He smiled, his eyes twinkling and the sunlight picking up greenish gold highlights in his hair.

"So, how is it that you're able to walk on land?" When he wrinkled his brow, she said, "I'm sorry if the question was rude."

"No. You're curious. I would be too." He lifted a large branch and moved it to an area at the end of her driveway she'd designated for larger debris. His muscles rippled and she wanted to forget about cleaning and take him inside. When he started to talk again, she struggled to remember what they were talking about.

"We gather as youngsters and learn to shift. To change our appearance. Some of our elders go and live with humans to learn your cultures. It helps us understand what land dwellers plan to do with the seas. Then they come back and teach the youngsters what they learned. Part of our lessons are to take turns shifting and playing with human children."

"Amazing. No one notices the difference?"

"Not really. You just say that your family is on vacation and no one bothers you." He moved closer, and together, they carried a large piece of siding to the pile.

"Do some of your people choose to stay on land and live as humans?"

"Not as many as you would think. Most of them can't wait to get back to the sea." He helped her set the siding down then stretched. "I understand why they would want to—the comfort of going home—but I like it on land. The sky, the sun." He reached out for her hand. "You."

"Well there is a lot more to dwelling on land than what you can learn on my beach. There are mountains, very high places that reach up into the sky. There are lakes filled with fresh water. There are deserts where there is no water at all."

Oh God, what was she doing, trying to tempt him to run off? Surely, he would rather explore. Better for him to know now and see if he's interested before he discovers there is more to life on his own and leaves when she's really attached. She grimaced and bent to pick up some Styrofoam cups. Dropping them into her bag, she waited for him to respond.

He grunted and stepped close, taking the bag from her hands. "Do you go to any of these places?"

"Not really." She clasped her hands together. "I mean, I've traveled, but there has always been something that draws me back to the coast."

"I wonder what it could be." He laughed and tossed the tied bags of garbage into the pile. Then he stepped closer and circled his arms around her waist. "We are the other half of each other."

A small voice in the back of her mind commented on how corny and unrealistic his words should have sounded. But that voice faded as she allowed herself to exist in that moment. They were bonded. She'd felt it happen. As if the clouds of the past few months parted, warmth bathed her in a sense of well being and hope for her future. She didn't need the statues or a financial boost from marrying well. She just needed him. The other half of herself. He kissed her forehead then walked to the deck steps and grabbed a water bottle. After taking a sip on the way back, he passed it to her.

A partner. She took a sip and caught his arm as he turned away. He needed to know how special he was to her.

"I don't know how this happened. I would never have thought this was possible." She blinked back tears that rose in her eyes. "I'm whole now."

With a whoop, he scooped her in his arms and spun her around. They laughed and kissed.

"Excuse me." A voice startled them apart. The mother from next door stood in front of Maggie's cottage. "Is the storm over this time?" Though she didn't say anything about him, she studied Tarman thoroughly.

Maggie stifled a giggle. *Can't blame her in the least.* "Yes, it's over this time. I still wouldn't allow the kids in the water until you hear the all clear on the news, but the storm has passed."

"Thank you." After looking Tarman over one more time, she walked back to her house.

Tarman slipped an arm around Maggie's waist. "Are you hungry? I could prepare a meal for us."

"Of course." She had no idea what he thought he could prepare. As far as she knew, he'd never used a kitchen appliance. But she had some calls to place, and it wouldn't hurt for him to make himself at home.

Inside, she left him in the kitchen. On her way to the studio, she could hear him humming. The melody was both strange and hauntingly familiar. She made it all the way into her studio before turning on her heel and striding to the kitchen door. He had his head in the refrigerator, occasionally lifting a container to his nose.

"What are you singing?" She didn't want to disturb him, but the quality of the song tickled her memory.

"Huh?" He turned to look at her, a package of cheese in his hand. "Oh, that. The whales sing it every year on their way back from their breeding grounds."

"Humpback whales?"

"Yes, I believe you call them that." He took a bag of grapes and a package of strawberries and set them on the counter beside the cheese. "They are very stolid creatures for the most part, but I can listen to their songs for hours."

Chapter Six

Maggie bit into a square of cheese. The meal consisted of finger foods, raw and bite sized. She ate slowly, enjoying his company and conversation. She learned more about the ocean in that hour than she could have learned in a lifetime in her house by the sea, or on the internet.

She found Tarman interesting and relaxing. Her home felt more like a home than ever. After they'd finished the food, they sat and watched the ocean out the front window. She rested her head on his shoulder.

The afternoon was perfect. She smiled. For the rest of her life, every afternoon would be perfect. "You know—" A car door slammed. "What was that?"

They both stood and went to the living room. Outside, Steve made his way toward the cottage. While they'd dated, the sight of him would make her knees go weak. After they called off the wedding, she dreaded seeing him again; afraid he could have the same power over her.

The man that walked up her driveway and took the porch steps two at a time was not the man she had dated, not the man to whom she had been engaged. Or rather, she wasn't who *she* used to be. Nothing he could say would make a difference in their situation, or how she would love Tarman for the rest of her life.

But she needed to handle Steve on her own so she asked Tarman to stand back. He brushed her cheek and walked into the bedroom, his expression unreadable.

Steve knocked—three sharp raps—then he opened it. "Maggs." The tone dripped humility. "Darling, I'm here to say I'm sorry. You are the only one for me." Only three steps into her house and the saccharine tone of his voice already churned her stomach.

"Maggs?" He turned and saw her. "Darling." He walked toward her, hands outstretched.

She didn't clasp them. "Steve."

"Oh, darling, don't be cold."

She sighed. "Things are over between us. You ended it when you slept with Angela."

"She means—"

"Nothing to you." She shook her head. "That's sad." She walked to the door and opened it. "I hope you find someone who does mean something to you."

"I did, Maggie. You mean everything to me."

"No I don't."

"I love you." His tone hardened along with his features.

"No you don't." She stepped out onto the porch, hoping he would follow. After a second, he emerged.

"I don't understand you." His face turned red around the ears. "You said you would marry me. Now just because of a mistake, you're going to go back on it? You're going to throw away two years?"

"Steve, we're not getting married. Your mistake was the best thing that could have happened." She smiled a little. "We aren't right for each other. At least we found this out before we made a permanent commitment."

She suspected he wouldn't take this well, but she hadn't anticipated the shade of maroon that now colored his face. She glanced over her shoulder, glad that she asked Tarman to stay out of the way.

"Oh no, you will not make a fool of me like you did at our rehearsal dinner." He grabbed her arm.

"You made yourself the fool, Steve."

He grabbed her other arm and shook her.

Never in the two years they'd been together had he laid a hand on her. She wouldn't have assumed he would. And of course, until now she'd never stood up to him. He simply couldn't take not getting his way. She tried to twist from his grip, but he held fast.

"Steve, you don't want to hurt me." She stopped struggling and tried to keep her voice calm.

"Oh, I don't know." He shook her again; an odd light entered his eyes. "Maybe I should have made sure you knew your place a long time ago. I thought you were a good one, but I see you need to learn proper respect."

"What?" Who the hell was this? She'd heard rumors about his previous relationships, but she hadn't given them credence. Now, as he shoved her down the stairs toward the inlet, she feared those rumors didn't scratch the surface.

Having no idea what he planned, she did the only thing she could think of. She dropped to her knees, rolling as soon as she came free from his grip. The light covering of water clinging to her from the still damp grass helped her avoid his grasp. His hands grabbed at her, but she eluded him.

Wriggling onto her back, she lashed out with her bare foot and caught him in the knee, the snap clearly audible over the waves pounding on shore. He howled. Instead of trying to get a hold on her slippery leg, he slammed his fist onto her shin.

Gasping in pain, she lashed out with the injured leg. Her heel caught him on the chin and sent him sprawling into the grass.

"Stop!" she screamed, scrambling away.

"Never." He picked up a rock and threw it at her. "I love you," he growled, clawing at the grass after her.

Tarman appeared and gripped Steve by the back of his shirt. He slipped one of his well-muscled arms across Steve's chest like a sash and lifted him off the ground. If she weren't so concerned, she would have laughed at the way Steve's arms flailed.

"Excuse me," Tarman said with a slight bow to Maggie. Then without another word, he took three steps and dove into the water, taking the still struggling Steve with him.

She stumbled to the water's edge in time to see Tarman's tail propel them away. Oh, God. What could she do? Who could she call? No one would believe her. She sat in the damp grass at the edge of the inlet, hoping she hadn't made another mistake in judging character.

* * * *

Tarman didn't take the squirming man very deep. Though he could push his thoughts into the man's mind, he needed light from the surface to make his point. Steve's eyes bulged as he stared at Tarman's tail. Tarman shook him.

"You need to leave Maggie alone." Tarman shook Steve again to punctuate his statement. "I don't want to see you around her again. If I do, I'll make sure you don't resurface." Steve's face started to change color. He needed to allow the man to breathe. "Am I understood?" If he didn't get a response, he'd have to change tactics.

Steve nodded vigorously. Tarman wasn't sure he could be trusted, but as the human started to turn blue, he really didn't have much choice.

They surfaced and Tarman hauled his burden to the shore beside Maggie's boat house. Tarman scanned the yard for her before tossing Steve onto the grass. She stood on the deck, wringing her hands. When she saw them, she ran over.

Flipping his tail, he propelled out of the water. He changed to human legs and landed near the coughing man. The injury on Tarman's leg sent fingers of pain shooting through the limb as he landed.

"Are you alright?" she asked. She grasped his arms.

Her concern delighted him. "I'm fine. Shouldn't have done that though, I'm not completely healed."

"Yes." She stepped back and considered him. "You should—"

He glanced down at himself. His shirt clung to his chest, but the remnants of his pants barely covered his naked human legs.

She'd worried over him, and like every female he'd ever known she was about to scold him for it. But the whimpering man at their feet cut her off. Steve coughed and crawled away. After about three feet, he staggered to his feet.

She took a step toward him and reached out a hand to steady him.

He yelped as if he'd been burned. "Stay away from me. Stay the hell away from me." His staggering increased speed as he fought his way up the hill and around the corner of the house. The engine of his car revved right before rocks from the gravel driveway clattered against the front of the cottage as he tore away.

* * * *

Maggie turned to Tarman who had the strangest smile on his face. "What did you do to him?"

"Nothing, really. I simply made him aware of what would happen if he didn't leave you alone." He took her hand and led her into the house.

Maggie couldn't let it go. "What if he calls the police?" She followed him into the bedroom. "He could make life very difficult for us."

Tarman removed his tattered pants, distracting her for a moment. She dug into the duffle bag and pulled out a pair of swimming trunks.

He put on the shorts then took both of her hands. "What would he tell them, my love? 'A merman took me underwater and threatened to drown me unless I leave my ex alone.' They wouldn't believe him for an instant."

She hadn't considered that. Anything resembling the truth would never be taken seriously. Lies would never stand up to scrutiny.

"I was so scared when you both went under."

"You feared I would drown?"

"It's a stupid human fear that you would somehow be hurt." She slapped at his arm.

"I have a fear." He gently pushed her backward until she sat on the edge of the bed.

"You do?" She recognized concern in his eyes but wouldn't have called it fear.

"Yes." He knelt before her. "I would like to make you my wife, but I'm afraid of your answer." He gazed into her eyes and waited.

Her first instinct was to compare Tarman's proposal to Steve's. But she pushed that memory away. The man in front of her loved her. They'd only met hours before, but they were meant to spend the rest of their lives together. He could only offer his love and companionship.

That was all she needed.

"I would love to marry you, Tarman." She placed her hands on either side of face. "I love you."

"I love you too, dear Maggie. I will all the days of my life." His arms circled her and held her close.

Epilogue

The beach was quiet as Maggie made her way to the water's edge. Labor Day weekend had come and gone, and most of the vacationers had left the area. Tarman said she should wait at the house and he would have his sister surface and dress in the boathouse. But Maggie shot the idea down. He'd been gone from his family for just over a year and she thought wading into the sea may be akin to meeting his sister halfway. More than anything, Maggie wanted to make a good impression on her sister-in-law.

She paced in the house the two hours Tarman said it would take to fetch his sister. Then, unable to wait inside another minute, she waded into the surf. A wave broke around Maggie's legs. Placing her hand on her rounded belly, she waded further into the water, turning her back to another wave.

A month ago, the motion of the waves would have made her ill. Now, the butterflies in her stomach had nothing to do with the life she carried, but with the one she was about to meet. Finally, the water to her right rippled and Tarman surfaced. Just behind him, another head appeared. The young face and bright smile matched the figure Maggie sculpted so long ago. Annalie.

She'd prepared for this for the past year. Maggie screwed up her courage and held out a hand to the mermaid. "It's so nice to meet you."

Annalie smiled wider and clasped Maggie's hand in both of hers. "You'll make a good match for Tarman."

The comment surprised and pleased Maggie, but she had to ask, "How can you tell?"

A female voice to Maggie's right said, "I've learned that Anna has a knack for judging character."

Maggie spun to find a woman standing beside her. The woman was familiar. "You're Tarman's mother." The Queen. *Oh my.*

"We'd like to visit a bit, dear." The queen embraced Maggie then backed up and laid a hand on Maggie's stomach.

"Of course." Maggie smiled.

Several more people arrived around her. She recognized all of them. Her husband's entire family surrounded her, and their faces sported friendly grins.

Tarman slipped a hand around her waist and led the way to the beach. "Once I was seen, my family ambushed me. Then they all wanted to come and meet you." He rubbed her arm. "I know you're nervous about this reunion, but they are so excited to meet you."

"No, no. I am fine with that now." She actually was. Especially with how obviously happy it made Tarman. One thing did still concern her. "It's just…do they have clothes?"

The End

Turbulent Hearts
By
Mae Powers

When Taroc rescues a beautiful alien woman from a watery death, the turbulent seas of his mind, heart, and body are enflamed by her completely. But will she reciprocate his feelings, or return to the sea of stars she fell from?

maepowers@yahoo.com

Digests with stories in them by Mae Powers:
Pagan Pleasures 2
Alien Seductions
Mélange
Jaded Destinies 1

Turbulent Hearts
By Mae Powers

Chapter One

Like a sleeping beauty, she lay in the coffin-like escape pod, only it was closed, and her mind and body were numb, while her body started becoming soaked. She felt the dampness around her, tingling her skin faintly. It seemed like she drifted on a turbulent ocean of endless waves. Dark, sporadic thoughts filtered through what consciousness she had left, and the lurking danger of insanity and drowning floated nearby.

She couldn't think coherently, the numbing from the low oxygen took over her body slowly. She hoped she died before she drowned. The metallic, oblong vessel that had become her coffin in space and now at sea, rocked within the waves, shifting her body side to side within the deadly enclosure.

Faintly, she recalled the meteorite shower which hit the side of the science vessel she worked upon for the last few months. Then the alarms went off and sections of the space ship started to explode. She vaguely remembered people running to the escape pods; those that hadn't already died in the first explosions. She'd been near one when a wave from an explosion in her sector sent her reeling against a wall. Dazed, she automatically dragged herself to the nearest escape pod. All she remembered was it closing over her and shooting out automatically from the ship. A planet loomed in her hazy mind and she went into blackness for a while.

Then she felt the bumps and heard and experienced the hard splash of the water when the pod landed. The rocking of thunderous splashing waves, and the water creeping into the cracked escape pod made her mind start to wake ever so slowly. She still couldn't move, couldn't think coherently more than a few minutes. She wished it would all end now, before the water sucked her down into its murky depths.

Just as she started to drift into unconsciousness again, she felt a sudden thump and then the coffin-crate stopped moving. It jerked to a dead halt, bumping her head side to side for a few deadly minutes.

Darkness engulfed her mind temporarily, then motes of light particles crashed in on the blackness. Irregular breathing spurts made her chest ache. She wanted to just sleep and never awaken again. But the fates had other plans for her, she believed. It seemed like hours went by and all she heard was the gentle wash of the waters splashing against the side of metal.

Something suddenly pounded on the outside of the pod. The noise broke through to her consciousness and then sounds of peeling metal screeched through her ears. The agony was soon replaced by light and darkness.

She hazily blinked and looked upwards as the metal was literally peeled back from the hatch of the pod. Above her she saw the night sky and a view of the stars filtering in as the wrecked hatch was peeled back even more. Then a shadowy face partially blocked out the night sky.

Soon, large hands pried her free of her former coffin. The being was large and her mind barely took in details of a gaunt face, dark green hair and the most incredibly beautiful star-gold eyes she'd ever seen. A worried look marred his handsome face for a moment. She reached up to touch his face and smiled.

"Thank you," she mumbled, before she lapsed into total, blissful unconsciousness this time.

* * * *

Torac had been enjoying his very early morning swim and floating on his back when he glanced up at the stars and saw the strange thing in the sky bearing down towards him. It splashed down with a vengeance in the water some distance away from him. Though he was a good and swift swimmer, it took him awhile to reach the thing. Dawn cracked by the time he arrived to check out the occurrence. Thankfully, he wasn't too far from the shore of a nearby island where some of his land-friends lived. It hadn't taken him long to reach the beach where the unusual object drifted to. The metallic-looking orifice looked large enough to hold someone of his length. With his sensitive hearing, he'd heard a groan coming from inside of the object.

Was someone trapped inside of it? Frantically he tried to find a way to open it. When he found what he thought was an indent in some kind of door, he jerked with all his strength to pull the thing open. The clear night sky enabled him to peer inside of it once he actually figured out he could get the mechanism open.

Seeing a body lying in there stunned him. Then acting with natural concern, he gingerly, but quickly pulled the person out of the object and lifted her up in his arms. He'd been surprised to see it had been a female. She had a shape similar to the land dwellers of this island.

Then she looked up at him with an odd expression and smiled just before uttering a few strange words. How had she gotten here, and in that device that fell from the sky? He knelt down with her in his arms, then laid her down some paces away from the pod. He left her a moment to look in side of it to make sure nothing else or no one else was in the strange thing.

He saw nothing of further note and went back to the female. Though he'd learned about healing, from his grandmother, it was mostly on sea-folk like himself that he helped from time to time. Torac softly straightened her legs and examined her the best he could.

He pushed her strangled hair out of her face, taking in her dark beauty. Her hair was darker than the sable sea-stones of this beach, while her bruised skin that wasn't covered by the strange outer skin-suit she wore looked the soft taupe coloring of the beach in the daylight. The stars were bright enough tonight, that when she was slightly coherent, he'd noted silvery colored eyes and dark pupils. An odd combination indeed, but she fascinated him.

She didn't look much shorter than him; and though she was slight of build, she purported all the lush curves a man could get lost in. He jerked himself out of his wayward thoughts and scooped her back up in his arms. It wasn't so late that his friend Persai would be asleep. Torac decided to take her there and see if his friend could take care of her until the two of them could figure out what to do. He'd known Persai and his wife for a long time and often, when not below the seas, in his natural habitat, he'd come exploring the island and visit the couple. They were kind and quite intelligent, so perhaps they'd know what to make of this strange beauty. Holding her close to his chest, he marched further inland.

Torac didn't have far to go, which was good for him. He couldn't stay out of the water more than a few hours or so each day. He looked down at the unusual beauty with her dark taupe skin and even darker hair. Definitely not of his world, but most certainly female. Her lush curves were not hidden well, but more defined in the outer skin-suit she wore.

He wondered what had brought her here. Persai, though of this world, had told him that there was life on other worlds besides Epauch. Although Persai hadn't left their planet, Minae, his wife had, for a year. During that time the female scientist had learned much, but didn't make a career of space travel. Not all Epauchians, she'd once told Torac, were able to stay for lengthy times in space; like seadwellers, they needed their roots on firm earth.

Torac understood that. His ancestors and people were undersea explorers, some land ones, but mostly undersea. They built large crystal cities below, keeping their distance from land dwellers that often were harmful to his kind. Not all Epauchians knew of space travel though. There were still barbaric tribes that fished in the waters where he lived and swam. Those are the ones he had to watch out for.

He wondered what kind of civilization this woman came from. Persai was born and raised on this island; his wife Minae came from a mountainous land far inland on one of the farther archipelagos she'd told him existed around Epauch. She'd traveled around the world of Epauch, finally coming here to Arataan, where she'd been part of an expedition of research explorers. After a few years, when the work had been done, she had chosen to stay; whereas most of the other team she worked with left for other places. Minae told him she hadn't wanted to leave though, since meeting Persai, and didn't miss her former life. She had helped the islanders to cultivate themselves more and to learn about their surroundings during her time here before and after she married Persai.

The people of the island weren't backwards but quite intelligent, though most preferred a simple lifestyle. They kept an open mind about things and knowledge, but knew also how to take care of and defend themselves should the need arise. They were by no means backwards people, here on the island but loved it here though and would do anything to protect their society should the need arise.

That was a good thing too, because on another island in the Seandrus Archipelago, there were fierce tribes that didn't get along with most of the other island peoples and especially sea-dwellers. He'd had his row with a few and his people, the Jnaith, stayed away from the more savage populace.

Finally, Torac saw the well-laid out village ahead. It's white-walled and brown thatched buildings of earth-stone were beautiful to see. Some were rounded, while others were more of the popular square type with long windows and doors and lovely patios. Tamperin was quite a large village compared to the bigger cities on Arataan's twin island Natiuk, just across the large bay from Arataan. For the most part, Torac didn't go to the similar laid-out island of Natiuk. Though a few small villages along its coastal lines were decent to the Jnaith, most weren't. Unlike Natiuk, all the islanders within the few villages and the one large city Arataan purported were friendly to the Jnaith. For the present, he was very glad of that fact, since he could come and go as he pleased to visit his friends here on Arataan.

He turned down one smooth pebbled street and within a few minutes he was at his friend's house. Persai was a healer and science learner, so his wife's knowledge of herbs and plants, plus her learnings from other places complimented Persai's abilities. The two were well-known on the island for their healing shop. In fact, his friends and a few villages like this one of Tamperin were the very few people that the Jnaith traded with, for anything.

Torac was glad Persai and Minae opened their shop during the early hours of the day. That's when people seemed to need medical attention the most around these parts, though most people on the island lived a healthy lifestyle, there were times his friends services and medicines were greatly needed.

"Torac, what have you brought…who have you brought this time…"

Minae saw him from the open window of the shop and rushed out to him. She fussed, telling him to bring the woman inside. Her small form, dressed in a flowing tunic of blue and green complimented the lively redhead. She'd always had a smile for him.

"Persai is in the city today. Quick bring her in the back, I'll close up."

He heard her bang the doors and windows shut, closing up the shop while he took the stranger to the back, where Persai's healing area stood. The room was warm and cozy, but clean and sterile at the same time. A table with some equipment upon it, a few chairs and a long bed-like bench for his patients to be examined upon were mostly the few sparse furnishings in the room. A few cupboards and shelves of various things also lined the room. A single window with curtains allowed sunlight into the room. It overlooked the sea less than a half mile where he'd found the strange female.

He laid her upon the cloth covered bench that barely held her long frame. He noticed upon closer inspection that she was not as slight as she felt or looked. The curves were there and he'd been more worried about getting her aid. Her front was undone a bit, showing ample cleavage. The more he stared at her lush dark hair, he noted coppery flecks in it, which gave her lovely face a more surreal look.

"Let's see who we have here and her condition." Minae came into the room. She took one look at him and grinned. "Interesting being, yes?"

He half smiled, nodding, then moved aside so his friend could examine the alien woman. "I know you don't always look over an ill person, but Persai says you can do some things. I trust you both."

"Well when I traveled in space, I was a base-medic, so I can tell a few things."

Having no doubt she could very well at least do that, he watched as she examined the woman slowly. "You think she's from space, Minae? Her clothing is like nothing I've seen before."

Minae took a moment to view the clothing the woman wore. She pointed at some insignia on the dark blue outfit. "Looks like a uniform of some kind. Where did you find her?"

"She was in some metal pod that fell from the sky into the sea, about a half mile from the village. I followed it ashore then pulled her out."

"Then it's more than likely she's from out there. In Kenta, where I'm from, we had a growing space fleet, but it was still within our solar system. There are not a lot of habitable planets around Epauch. We may have someone that's from way out there, Torac."

He shook his head at the wonderment of it. "So you never met any strange aliens in your short travels?"

She shook her head negatively, then looked up at him. "No. She looks more bruised than anything, perhaps a little internal stress. I'm going to clean her up with some healing ointment. That will help her until Persai comes back tonight. Leave her with us for the next few days, she'll be fine. You can't stay out of the water too long."

"True. I will leave her in your capable hands then. I'll come back by tomorrow tonight then and visit with you when Persai is home. Thank you, Minae."

He had wanted to stay, but Minae was right, he couldn't be out of the water more than a few hours at time. There wasn't much he could do here but get in the way; and to take up Minae's company while she tended to the unusual beauty would be a waste of both their time. Thankfully his long strides would get him back to the beach quickly just as he'd gotten here so fast while carrying the alien woman.

He gave Minae a quick press on the shoulder with his left hand, which was the villager's customary touch for a friend, then left to go to the ocean. All the time though, he thought of the strange beauty and wondered who indeed she was; but more so, where she came from.

Perhaps, he thought, *I'll find out tomorrow night.*

Chapter Two

"A meteorite shower hit our ship. I was lucky to escape," Darea told the two people sitting across from her at the small kitchen table.

The woman was a lively redhead with pale skin and wore a green and blue tunic, while the tall, thin man, introduced as Persai, Minae's husband, sat dressed in a brown tunic and trousers. His brown eyes glancing over her contemplatively, Darea knew the alien man kept watch on her for medical reasons. She'd been told he was a healer. Not a regular doctor like she was use to, but a psychic healer who could cure almost anything with his mind or touch of a hand. Her body felt alive, she was sure due to these two people and the being who'd rescued her from the escape pod.

It was early evening, but she'd been awake for the better part of the afternoon now. She took it easy the first few hours upon arising, though she'd felt fine and able to sit up. She'd been unconscious for nearly a day, they told her, but was recovering swiftly. Whatever Persai and Minae did to heal her worked fast, for which she was glad of. Still, she had a few aches and finally became famished. She didn't know how long she'd been out there in the pod, drifting around. Darea just knew she was thankful to be alive after the ship's explosion and then the pod making it through Epauch's atmosphere and near this island.

She felt even luckier to have been rescued by these kind people. Now she wondered what she was going to do. She glanced at the couple looking at her speculatively and asked. "Did this friend of yours who rescued me, Taroc, see any other pods drop from the sky?"

She didn't want to assume they were uncivilized or unknowledgeable about space travel when she first met them. From their intelligent faces and the tools they had around the room, she didn't think they were without some knowledge of scientific know-how. And the fact that Minae had said she space-traveled for a year gave way to the fact there were some on Epauch who understood advanced knowledge.

Minae pushed back the cup of warm brew they'd all been drinking and Darea found she liked. It had been soothing, she believed medicinal for her. The two looked at each other then glanced back at her before Minae spoke up again.

"I don't think so. Did you hear of any thing like that in the city when you were there yesterday, Persai?"

He shook his head. "I heard nothing about any strange pods landing around this area. No one mentioned it. That don't mean others didn't land somewhere else around Epauch."

Minae lightly ran a finger around the rim of her cup. "There's a way to find out. I have a communications device that will let me speak with others from my old crew. I'm from a more advanced area of Epauch originally, Darea. Like I mentioned about an hour ago, when we told you about Epauch, the city I was raised in had a center for space studies and training. That translator medallion I gave you came from there."

Darea fondled the gold and red star-shaped medallion Darea had given her about an hour after awakening. It wasn't perfect in its translations, but they were doing nicely about understanding each other. Besides being an exobiologist, she'd also been great at easily translating alien linguistics, so started picking up their language quickly with the help of the translator necklace. She was sure it wouldn't take her long to learn the language, it being similar in some ways to an old language not unlike from her native home-world. Perhaps, in time, if she did contact someone from her planet, they could exchange knowledge and customs. It's what her people strived for. She just wished others from her lost ship were here now.

"I hope some did survive," she mumbled, fondling the necklace, and twisting the center dial on it to better pick up words from them.

"There's still the chance some of your people may have landed on other parts of Epauch," Persai reiterated.

"There is, and I hope so," Darea replied. "This was our first foray into your part of the galaxy. Our solar system is several light-years from your own. We were exploring a planet we named Labada-8. It wasn't habited but had some extremely wonderful plant species which we discovered had medicinal purposes."

Minae jerked her head upwards. "Did this world have some tall thin green and purple plants with green and yellow leaves about four feet in diameter?"

Darea blinked her eyes, assimilating Darea's question. "Yes, as a matter of fact it did. Did your crew travel there?"

The other woman nodded. "Yes, that particular plant, which we named Starmas, is being grown in Fentwi, the city I grew up in, and here in our backyard herb garden. It has remarkable properties for healing most anything and has been thoroughly tested. The world you called Labada-8 is uninhabited except for some plant and a few animal species that are quite docile. Heavens, that means your people might have met mine. This is quite remarkable."

"Your Professor Havendor would love to meet with, Darea," Persai stated. "Your race is similar in physical qualities to our own, Darea. Was your family on board at all? Friends? Perhaps there is a way we can contact your world if Professor Havendor is let in on your being here. What do you think, Minae?"

Minae looked from her husband, brushed her hair back with one hand then contemplated that question. "I could arrange a meeting with my old teacher. He would be delighted, I'm sure to meet with you, I'm sure. Not in any of the space travels our people have attempted have we met someone from another world. We haven't gone any further than the planets at the edge of our own solar system. Epauch is fourth from our sun, and there are only seven more until our solar system ends, but only three of them are habitable and the one you visited we called Nataba. I know the Space Academy and

Science Center in Fentwi had planned more trips there and perhaps eventually beyond our solar system."

"The planet I am from is called Urtha. My race has been doing space exploration for nearly a hundred years now. We've come a long way and our world's nations are peaceful with one another, so space travel became a goal for all concerned on our world. We too have not yet came across another planet with life forms like our own, or anything similar to yours even. The ridges around your ears are perhaps the only dissimilar notations that I see right now, but you're as humanoid as my race is. The people around my world have different hair and physical colorings, plus cultural differences, but humanoid still. What about here?"

"We have variety here too," Minae explained. "There are also, some amphibian cultures here. Like Taroc's. His people are aquatic and live mostly below the sea, coming up for air several times a day and are only able to stay out of the water a few hours a day. They are pretty advanced though they have not space traveled yet."

"Incredible. We've just discovered ancient underwater civilizations on Urtha. Perhaps my ancestors knew Taroc's."

"Or it's just a coincidence that your world has amphibianoids too," Persai said. "As far as I know, Taroc's people never space traveled. We'll have to ask him, Minae."

"He's never mentioned they have, Persai, whenever I've asked him about his race's history. They are one of the oldest races on Epauch and he doesn't quite know all their historical data, I believe."

At that moment, they heard a rap on the outside of the main door. Persai jumped up.

"It is probably Taroc. I'll bring him in." Persai left to go into the main room of the house.

"I have been curious to meet him, Minae. I really must thank him for saving my life and bringing me to you. I will never be able to thank you and Persai enough."

Minae smiled and patted Darea's hand. "You've thanked me enough. I am glad you did drop into our lives. I've been wanting to see my old professor again to catch up on the latest finds, and you're just the incentive I've needed to get moving in that direction. Ah, the rescuer is here."

Smiling, Darea turned and her heart started thumping erratically when she espied the tall man coming up behind Persai, into the room. He was taller than her recollection of him; yet, he still had that lustrous dark green hair and the most incredible star-gold eyes she'd ever seen. Not that she'd seen many people with such startling eye coloring before. In fact, he was the only one she recalled seeing with such bright star-gold eyes. Eyes framed by long, black lashes that stared at her intently.

She found him very appealing however, on several levels. He looked as humanoid in most ways as did Minae and Persai. Even with Taroc's webbed feet and long nailed fingers, he was very much a male. His athletically muscled body pleased her feminine senses very much. So much in fact, she had a hard time keeping her eyes off his appealing form. Darea had the feeling he knew that too.

His full lips curved upwards to see her staring at him. She felt herself blush slightly and knew he had been studying her as much as she'd been scrutinizing him. She quickly composed herself as Persai and her rescuer fully entered the large kitchen-workroom of Persai's and Minae's house.

"As you can see, Taroc, our guest is recovering quite fast and well." He pulled out a chair next to his wife. "Taroc, this is Darea. The translation medallion has helped her to understand out language, but I believe she would comprehend it quite well without it. She told Minae and I that she's a linguist as well as a scientist. Please sit."

Taroc did so, and near Darea. "I am pleased to see you are recovering."

Darea cleared her throat and her thoughts. "Thank you for pulling me out of the pod. I never thought to see daylight again, or be alive. The pod felt like a coffin."

"Well dry land is beneath you now and this island is very good for the soul and recovering. You may stay here as long as you like, Darea," Minae said.

"I hope you take them up on that invitation, Darea." Taroc seconded that notion. "The people her are very friendly even when curious."

"I've no doubt that word will spread soon about our visitor," Persai stated. "I believe Professor Havendor might be a good call. He would know if any others from your ship survived."

"I'll communicate with him tomorrow mid-morning. If I recall correctly, he's usually in his study then at the Science Center. Would that be agreeable with you, Darea?"

She was at a loss still in some ways because of what had happened to her and her shipmates, but anxious too to find out word about the crew of her destroyed ship. "Yes, I think that would be the best course of action. Thank you all for everything."

"I'm glad we could help you out. Isn't that right, Taroc?"

Taroc, she noted, hadn't been able to take his eyes off her. "Er, yes, quite right."

"Perhaps you'd like to take Darea for a stroll along the beach. It's cool out there now and I think some fresh air would do her good, don't you, Persai?"

Persai chuckled. "Absolutely."

"I think I can handle that. You'll be safe with me, Darea."

Well at least his words promised that even if his eyes didn't, Darea mused. Yet, she wanted to have time to think and perhaps a stroll along the beach would help clear the cobwebs in her mind. She also couldn't deny she wanted to thank Taroc personally for saving her life by rescuing her from the pod and the turbulent waters that nearly had been her doom.

She stood up with the others. "I think I'd like that."

"Don't keep her out too late, Taroc," Minae admonished. "We do get up early around here."

He smiled and bent to kiss Minae's cheek, as an old friend might do to one they were fond of. "Yes, Minae. I shall bring her back safely and not too late."

He offered Darea his arm and after she took it, he winked at Persai but said nothing more as he led Darea out of the house. Darea kept from blushing again, but knew she felt giddy about being alone with Taroc. The amphibianoid did strange things to her system. But Darea didn't mind at all right that moment. She needed the distraction. It'd been a while since she had been alone in an attractive male's company. No harm could come of that fact. Of course, with him at her side, sensual trouble just tempted the hell out of her.

Chapter Three

Torac wanted to visit Persai and Minae sooner, but had duties he needed to take care of at his underwater home. Being the son of an undersea city-governor, and next in line for the inherited position, he had to help his older brother and father take care of ruling the crystal dome city where they resided. It wasn't that he wanted to shirk his duties, but upon rescuing the alien woman, she was all that filled his mind.

Holding her in his arms had been strange for him. He'd had female companionship that was more than pleasing, but something about the unusual dark beauty just tugged at his sensual strings more than any other woman had before. His brother Jeth noted it last night at dinner, his preoccupation. But when asked, he evaded the issue.

How did one tell his siblings he might have found his sea-mate? Especially since they expected him to marry another sea-governor's daughter to tighten the city-holds more. Expected, yes, but he did not believe they would force him into a loveless marriage. He loved the twin crystal cities of Barras and Varnos, but he also liked the freedom of coming and going as he pleased and to visit the upper lands above the turbulent seas of the underwater realms.

His siblings and sea-faring friends didn't quite understand his passionate fascination for land dwellers and the realms above the Epauchian seas. But they more than tolerated his need to go above the water worlds. For Persai saved his life when a young lad, and afterwards, a trade pact had come about once sea folk of Barras and Varnos found out about it and how friendly the island people of Arataan were. Plus the land dwellers were honest, hardworking folk and that appealed to the people of his undersea world. For nearly twenty years they'd been friendly with each other. And a few years back, when Minae and friends from her old home had helped to vanquish some savage pirates from destroying Taroc's undersea realms, all concerned were strengthened in their ties of trade and friendship.

In a sense, Taroc was an ambassador for the trading aspects of Arataan and some of the islands, between them and the sea domains. He liked his position, it allowed him plenty of visiting Minae and Persai and others he knew on the islands. He did not think anything would perturb the peace of most of the Seandrus Archipelago peoples and that of his own sea-race. He'd do his damnest to see that never happened.

He wondered if the alien woman would be trouble for his sea-lands or not, or for his heart, for that matter. Taroc wasn't sure why, but his instant attraction for her disturbed him. He'd learned early in manhood, that sea-males knew instinctively right away when they would meet their sea-mate. The aquatic females had this ability too, but not to the extent that the men did. But he'd never know, so far, of a sea dweller and a non-aquatic being ever uniting.

Perhaps he was just getting ahead of himself and his libido. After the first concerns of finding the woman were over and knowing she was safe, he'd really studied her while he carried her to Minae's and Persai's dwelling. He'd been fascinated with the strange beauty as well as concerned for her well-being. However, upon seeing her again and fully awake, her loveliness and sensual aura took his heart and body by surprise.

But that wasn't an unwelcome factor, just a confusing one to his mind and body. And now, as they silently walked side-by-side, his inner senses felt content, as if this was meant to be. Again, though, he realized his emotions and needs were getting ahead of him. He wasn't sure how she'd respond to any amorous advances, despite the fact he'd felt her looking him over in an appreciative way. No, old-fashioned courting was the way for now.

The trail from his friends abode led them to a small lagoon, which he'd traipsed around when he'd first brought her into the village. The lagoon was deep at this part, but further lead into the sea and ended near the beach where he'd found her pod. He hadn't realized they had enjoyed the quiet companionship for nearly a quarter of an hour.

Taroc glanced over at her and stopped when she did to glance up at the stars, for it had turned slightly dark and the stars started to awaken just after dusk came. She stood glancing down at the water before she turned her lovely face up at him.

She searched his eyes for a few minutes before she spoke. "I want to thank you very much for pulling me out of the pod."

He smiled warmly down at her. Though he was only a few inches taller than her right now she seemed very vulnerable. He supposed it was from feeling at a loss with her surroundings and unsure what she would do with her life now. When the time arose, he'd ask her what she intended to do with herself; after she had time to assimilate her own thoughts on the subject.

"I wondered what you said to me just before you passed out."

She gave him a half grin. "Thank you. I wasn't too coherent, but I knew I was glad to get out of that pod."

He gave her a reassuring smile in return. "You look so much better now."

"I feel alive again, which is a good thing." She turned briefly to look at the water, then the stars and back at him before she spoke again. "Minae and Persai are wonderful people. Fascinating too. As is your world, well what I've seen of it. On Urtha we do not have aquatic races. What is it like to live beneath the ocean? I've explored my planet's seas and studied amphibian life, but never met a sea person before."

Taroc chuckled but didn't move any nearer to her than he already was. Not that he didn't want to reach out and touch her lovely face and stroke it as tenderly as she briefly did his a day ago after rescuing her.

"Beneath the sea near here are two crystalline cities which part of the Jnaith sea race lives within. There are some other cities scattered in other oceans around Epauch, but the two below the seas around here are twin cities called Barros and Varnos. I come from Barros. The many colors of flora and reefs below are reflected in the near-transparent structures making it look like an iridescent rainbow of structures. It is a wondrous sight to behold, by anyone."

"I can tell you love the ocean, perhaps as much as Minae loves Persai and this island."

"You're very astute. She is at home here and is devoted to Persai and this island. And yes, I do love the oceans. Like traveling in space, I suppose, freedom to go anywhere."

"I always wanted to visit the stars, but since you can breathe beneath an ocean, I'd say you have more freedom to do as you wish. Space ships can be confining when shared with a large crew. But if I could breathe underwater, I would love to see what your city looks like. It sounds dreamy and fascinating."

"I believe you would like it very much." He took a tentative step towards her, relieved when she did not back away. "If you could breathe underwater, I'd take you there now, or when you felt up to it."

Darea smiled up at him but didn't move any closer. "I'd like that. It must be incredible for you to both breathe in and out of the water. If there were a way, I'd definitely take you up on that offer."

He looked deeply into her silvery tinted eyes. "Perhaps there is a way, if you're sure."

She took a step nearer to him. "How so?"

"Some of my race has extra sensory abilities. Amongst them are memory-share sensations. I could share images of my experiences with you and you'd feel them as I did. You would have to let me join my emotional mind to yours."

She cocked her head to one side, as if in contemplation, yet there was a seductive half-smile on her full lips. "I feel I can trust you, after all you did save my life."

He felt elated and took the last few steps to be skin-to-skin next to her. "You are safe with me. You have but to say stop and I will pull you back up to reality."

Darea chuckled softly, pressing close to him. "Being here is a bit unreal. But I'm receptive to you. Please go ahead."

Taroc leaned in towards her and placed his hands on either side of her face. He touched his forehead to hers then closed his eyes. Slowly, ever so slowly, he gently seeped into her mind with his, letting visions of his world flow sweetly into her consciousness.

* * * *

A colorful mix of iridescent blue, green, and purple waters swirled around in her mind and then in her body. She felt as if he dove down deep with her in his arms, showing her all the wonders of his undersea world. Crystal-like structures appeared to rise before them. Towers tenderly sculpted in breathtaking architecture took her breath away almost as much as the water could have.

Beings and creatures of soft blues, browns, and other wondrous colors swam in and around the buildings and mountains below this fantastic turbulent sea of life. Natural luminescence from corals and underwater mounds that had plant life around them illuminated the whole depth of this marvelous place. She wanted to explore every iota of this watery kingdom.

From his mind into hers he told her what was what: names of living and non-living things all around them. She could almost reach out and touch the fantastic scenery around her. In fact, she could feel the motions of what his mind showed her. It truly all was the most wonderful sights and sensations she'd almost ever experienced. She's seen marvels in space and even in the oceans of her own home-world, but this all still was so incredibly beautiful and uplifting to one's spirits.

With such a unique and lovely place, one could almost never wish to leave it. Calm and inviting but full of adventurous life and almost indescribable beauty, it was an underwater heaven of bliss.

He showed her his life in flashes into her mind, things he experienced and lived through as a child and young adult, all up through the time he'd been swimming and saw her pod. She marveled at how he could swim with such ease beneath the seas and with such incredible speed over them.

She felt invigorated and part of his life, his world. She opened her mind further to him and without hesitation she shared her feelings back with him. Darea felt him tremble beside her and his arms tighten around her body. In her own mind, she could feel him experiencing her own life, the sights of her world, and the sight of him coming to her rescue. And of what she felt when she laid eyes upon him again.

She sighed within his arms and then suddenly felt him slowly bring her back to their present realm. That, she felt, had truly been one of the most ecstatic times of her life. Troubles ebbed at her about her future, but in his arms, she somehow felt as if she could handle whatever turbulent times came her way.

Darea laid her head against his wide chest. She sighed, feeling content. She had some empathy abilities, but not to the extent of what he'd just shared with her. Now he knew most of what she felt and thought, as she did his own feelings and views. Her heart and mind opened to new possibilities now.

Tomorrow, she felt, she'd know more of what she would do; of how the two of them might…just might be able to discover more within each other. But for now, and she felt it within him, they were content to just hold each other.

Much later, after he walked her back to Minae's and Persai's cottage, he pulled her softly into his arms and glanced deeply into her eyes, as if studying her very soul. She quivered at the intensity of the feelings she felt emanating from within him and encompassing her.

"You are an incredible person, Darea. I've never felt such wondrous fulfillment of sharing my mind-feelings with another."

She smiled up at him. "Nor I another. I have empathic tendencies, but what I felt out there, tonight in your arms, was definitely one of the most incredible things I've ever experienced. Thank you for sharing all that with me."

"My pleasure also." And to her surprise, he leaned down and gently kissed her cheek. "Inside with you. I need to get back in the water. I shall come by tomorrow if you like."

"I'd like that very much." She was glad the moonlight kept him from seeing her blush. She smiled at him and turned to go into the cottage, looking forward to the next day.

Chapter Four

"I do believe he's smitten, Minae." Persai grinned in between bites of his breakfast morsels.

Minae loved Persai's lopsided grin; it was one of the sweet and sexy physical qualities that drew her to him. His eyes glittered with lively amusement. Sexy eyes, she thought. They still showed a lot of love for her even after several years of marriage. All females should be as lucky, she mused.

"I've never seen him perk up so much, that's for sure. Especially in any other female's presence. I think you're right, dearest."

"Of course I am," he chuckled. "Not often I'm wrong, you know. Except when we agree you are."

She laughed warmly and openly. "Of course. Thanks for cooking this morning, you out-did yourself."

"Thank you." He put his eating utensil down and looked upon her with such loving warmth she wanted to grab his hand and lead him back into their bedroom. "Now, about Professor Havendor's coming; I know you called him earlier this morning. He did confirm, correct?"

She nodded. "Definitely. They are taking a fast air-transport to the main island west of here, then will arrive with our village's trade supplies from the mainland tomorrow morning. He said he had some interesting developments but didn't want to say much until he arrived. That's about all we'll be able to let Darea know right now."

He pushed his plate forward a bit, which he did when he was done eating. "I think that will give her some hope, but she'll probably still be a little anxious until tomorrow."

Minae touched her napkin to her lips, wiped off her hands, and put her own dish to one side. "I agree. But it will be nice to have her here. She's a unique person."

"You like her, don't you? Like me, you've always been able to use your intuition to determine a person's character. And I've always trusted your judgments."

She reached across the small breakfast-nook table and squeezed his hand. "Thank you, love. Yes, I do like her. She's open and honest. Reminds me of you in some ways, her character traits that is."

"She's lovely and a good person. Not as beautiful as you of course, but pretty enough to catch Taroc's interest."

Minae leaned back in her seat and sighed. "I don't know that we should encourage that aspect, Persai. She might want to leave with her people, if any survived."

"If they have no ship to leave in, then that's really not a problem. Unless Professor Havendor has notified your old space center to the effect of aliens being here amongst us."

She looked up at him, cocking her head to one side. "Well there is that." Then she laughed lightly, studying him. "No, I have no interest going back to other worlds. It would be interesting to see if our world has a curiosity in contacting hers. Or more perhaps, they might do an expedition to her world. First contact and cultural exchange has long been a dream to some of our races."

"It would be an intriguing possibility. I often wondered what lay out there."

Her eyes widened a bit. "You never told me you thought about going out there, just had some inquisitiveness about it."

"I think I was being a bit petrified of what or who was out amongst the stars. If others who are as amenable as Darea are out there, perhaps the possibility is just that much more inviting."

Smiling, she nodded in agreement. "I can see that aspect. It is scary at first and contact with a new species can be intimidating. Who knows, perhaps we might consider it later on. Hmm?"

He gave a slight nod and was about to answer her when they both heard light footsteps. Turning around, both saw Darea coming into the kitchen, shuffling half asleep to their breakfast nook.

She looked a little disheveled, as if she'd had a hard time sleeping. They'd loaned her a robe of Persai's whom she was closest to in height and the light blue robe was a bit rumpled.

She pulled back one of the other empty chairs, grinning. "Sorry I'm a bit late for breakfast. I didn't fall asleep until the wee hours."

"I'll fuss at Taroc later for keeping you out so late."

Darea put a hand through her locks and tousled them. "That's not necessary. Taroc was a perfect gentleman. We had a lovely walk. Besides being troubled over what has happened to my ship and crewmates, I think I'm a bit anxious for news from your Professor Havendor."

Minae promptly told her what substantial information she'd gotten from the professor. "So he'll probably be here about mid-morning tomorrow."

"It will give me time to visit with you both, perhaps see your town. That's if you think it will be ok."

Minae nodded and glanced at her husband before speaking to the alien beauty. At his slight nod, she spoke. "I think that can be arranged. Here, you get something to eat first. I'll round you up some more clothing and afterwards you can clean up. Give it an hour and we'll both be glad to take you into town."

Minae watched the woman curiously, as she nibbled slightly. She could tell the alien female was still troubled over her loss and being on a strange world. Perhaps an outing would brighten her day. She'd make sure to get a smile on Darea's face. Or perhaps Taroc could. She steered away from that thought and how best to help the woman.

* * * *

Darea had a nice time seeing the small town, escorted by her new friends. Minae and Persai showed her different places of interest; like the oldest temples on the island, the cliffs near the edge of the town not far from the docks where supply ships came in, and several of the shops they frequented.

Many people seemed to know them, for they all waved to the couple in a friendly manner. Though others seemed curious about her, they did not deliberately stop to inquire about who she was. Although the people came in different sizes, shapes, and colors, she knew she was more exotic than the islanders were with her darker skin coloring and soft sable hair.

Minae had mentioned that before they went out, that people would see her differently but not in a bad way. She said others from her home-city had varying colors of skin tone, shapes, hair and eye colorings; so there Darea would have fit right in. The only exception being her silvery eyes, which Minae said were very unique in coloring and quite beautiful.

Darea liked her new friend, thankful that Persai and Minae were kind enough to take her in. She felt wistful and sad still, but hope lay within her that some of the others from her ship had survived. If not, she would be making a new life here on this world. But she would not worry about that until she heard from Professor Havendor.

Temporarily setting her troubles aside, she tried to enjoy her outing as best she could. The large village bustled with life and quaint buildings. She could see why her benefactors loved the place. For Minae to leave a large city of technology for a remote island must have been a severe change. Yet, by the way Minae and Persai often looked at each other so lovingly, Darea believed Minae never regretted coming to this paradise.

After having lunch at an open sidewalk restaurant, and then doing some slight shopping, the trio headed back down to the town's edge where Minae's and Persai's abode lay. Their area was not far from the lagoon and sea or beach upon where her pod had washed ashore. She could understand why they liked their privacy too, though they had a healing shop and small medical facility in front of their house.

Some of their home, too, was a workshop of sorts, though the cottage felt like a home where anyone would love to live. Darea had always loved exploring and had not yet decided where or when she'd like to settle down at, if that ever happened to her. She knew one day she would tire of space traveling, but had not considered it would happen for a while yet in her life.

Perhaps, if she found what these two had, she would more than likely think upon settling down. Time would tell if she would be lucky enough to find a man she found worth giving up the stars for. But it made her think of Taroc as they walked homeward. He was unlike any other male she had ever met. Exotic and sexy, and very tender. His feelings shown honestly in his handsome face and that she admired very much about him. It also stirred long-dormant needs within her whole body and mind.

Part of her was drawn to his enigmatic nature, but she also felt as if she needed to hold herself back until she found out what the morrow would bring. She couldn't very well think about a life here until she knew if any of the others survived; could she?

She sighed and quietly followed the couple back to their home. There wasn't much she could do, of course until she saw what tomorrow brought. Inwardly, she hoped Taroc did visit again today as he said he would. She wasn't sure why, but it meant a lot to her that he did. Darea did not think she could take it if he didn't.

When they finally arrived, the couple went to put away their packages and she took advantage of some time alone in their study that lay at one side of the kitchen workshop at the front of the house, not far from the entrance to their medical healing shop.

For a few hours, she busied herself with researching Epauch through the computer-like terminal that Persai and Minae had told her she could use. She was glad she had not landed in a more rustic, less technological place. She'd seen various technological gadgetry around the island town, so was glad when earlier, before they left to go on their outing, Minae had told her they had an older computer system in their home that they used for various research and communications to other areas of the planet. Persai had shown her what the symbols meant, and she felt she could pick up things fairly quickly.

She consulted the translator necklace when she had to; but for the most part, she amazed herself how quick and easy it was to pick up the general main language that the islanders had used. She'd noted various dialects and Minae pointed out that the townsfolk were a mixture of different races from around Epauch, though at least half of them were island natives.

Darea made use of her time, learning about some of the culture not only on the island but around the planet, garnering as much as she could at once. She knew she couldn't learn it all in one day, but with her photographic memory, she picked up a lot of information. She studied the main dialect for at least an hour and downloaded some more phonics and words into the necklace piece, as she learned how to do it on their net-system.

Though there were quite a few advances in Fentwi, where Minae came from, her race was still more advanced. It helped her now to learn the aspects of Epauchian life. culture and technology that she needed to know. Her brain was filled with a lot of information when she shut off the system about four hours later. She needed some refreshment, something cool to drink.

She made her way back to the kitchen area and helped herself to a cool drink from their food cooling unit. Once done she sat down at the table to enjoy her beverage. She toyed with the necklace lightly then when she heard footsteps approaching, then quickly looked up.

True to his word, Taroc had come. Her heart beat faster at seeing the amphibian humanoid in all his splendor. He wore a sleeveless tunic shirt of cream and brown that matched the khaki shorts he wore. It showed off his muscled form very pleasingly. Her feminine urges soared at his appealing appearance.

He wore no shoes, with his slightly webbed feet, but she liked his handsome features nonetheless. And his sexy smile. It made her heart beat faster. His star-gold eyes sparkled with an intensity she quickly realized was interest in her as a woman, perhaps more.

"I'm glad you came today," she said, her voice a bit breathless.

She stood up as he approached. "So am I. Would you care to go for a swim with me? They do swim on your world, don't they?"

She nodded. "Yes, we do. Give me a moment and I'll let Minae know."

He smiled at her. "Good, I need a few words with Persai. I saw him in the backyard upon my arrival. I'll meet you back here shortly."

Darea agreed, but upon leaving, she had the feeling he watched her until she was out of sight. Minae was in the shop, though this morning the woman told her it was the day they closed it to the public.

Minae smiled but inquired with her lovely eyes. She had such knowing eyes, too; Darea didn't think she could keep much from the woman, but then she had no desire to. Minae had been an instant friend to her, which Darea would always cherish.

"If you don't mind, I'm going to go for a walk and swim with Taroc. He's out back now talking with Persai."

Minae studied her a moment. "Enjoy yourself, perhaps we can talk when you get back."

Darea wondered if something was wrong, but chucked it up to the thought that Minae was just looking out for her. "I'll be fine. Thank you again for a lovely morning. I shall not be out too late this time, so no need to worry."

Darea left quickly but had the feeling Minae would worry anyway. She shrugged off the offish feeling and prepared as fast as she could to go on her jaunt with Taroc.

Chapter Five

They walked quietly together until they reached the beach. Last night he'd taken her to the lagoon, which was just a few minutes away from this beach area, and in particular where her escape pod had washed ashore.

She started to look at him when she noticed the pod was still on the beach, not far from the water. For some reason she had to go see it, perhaps to put it out of her mind how she got here, she wasn't sure, just that she had to see it. Without word to him, she quickly headed to the pod.

Once there she realized he came up behind her. She just stood there in silence for a moment before she turned to look up at him. "I just had to see it, I guess."

He reached out and stroked her cheek softly. "Go ahead, take what time you need."

She smiled warmly up at him and then turned back to the pod. It was oblong and dented, made of a dark gray metal, a good thick metal that helped to keep her alive. In her case, technology was a good thing. She moved tentatively at first the last few steps towards it, then knelt down and peered into the opening. It was wide and jagged though the door to the pod was pulled severely back.

Darea realized the amphibianoid's physical strength when she saw the mangled door. The trip may have dented and jagged it quite a bit, but he had to have ripped it open to be as it was right now. She peered inside. There was nothing in there but a fairly large emergency pack she knew were standard issues for these escape pods. She reached in and pulled the pack out. She set it down on the pod top and then ruffled through the thick clothed bag.

Yes, medical supply kit, rations, a solar blanket, a few miniature emergency tools, a unisex jumpsuit that would stretch to fit almost any size, and a communicator. None of it looked broken or harmed. She pulled out the square gray communicator and twirled it in her hands.

Darea sat on a good solid part of the pod near the emergency pak then looked up at Taroc, who eyed her curiously. "It's a small but, long-range communicator from my world. It seems to be working. Well I hope it does."

"Persai said the professor was due tomorrow, but did not say if any of your people were with him. You must be curious. I would not blame you if you called to see if you can communicate with anyone."

She rubbed her chin. "I want to, yet I guess I'm a little scared to. Perhaps shortly. I think right now, I could use that swim. I'm too tense, too jittery to know what to say or who to contact."

He reached out his hand. "I think I would be too. Let's go swim. I'm sure it will relax you and then you can decide what to do."

She nodded and took his hand. He helped her up and then reached for the pack. She gave him the communicator to put inside it.

"It can wait a few more minutes. I'm glad you brought me here though. I'd forgotten about this being in here. It's standard issue."

"I'm glad we came then. Come, let's leave it in the pod for now, and go swimming in the sea, not the lagoon."

She pulled off the robe dress she had on and his eyes widened at seeing her in the one-piece tank swim wear she had on. Chuckling she tried not to blush.

"Minae said it was what some women wear when they bathed in those public pools you have here or the sea. She purchased this one for me today when we were out touring the village."

"That blue suits you. It is very appropriate and flattering too. Uhmm, shall we swim then?"

She chuckled again and let some tension ease off. She would use the communicator, but for right now, she wanted time with him. It might be their last chance to do so and she knew she had to be with him. Her heart tightened a bit, but she shrugged off the uneasiness once more and walked with him into the water.

* * * *

Taroc admired her form in the water; she swam as gracefully and powerfully as any female of the Jnaith race. Yet, he enjoyed her splashing and stroking through the water a lot more. Her body was built for lovemaking and treasuring. The thought startled him as he splashed around with her near the beach.

In such a short time, he realized she had pierced the coolness of his heart. No other female had ever gotten so close to his tender feelings before. He always knew what he wanted from a woman, but this exotic beauty seeped into his very being in all ways.

He tried hard not to think about those stronger feelings as they swam and relaxed in the deeper waters. He'd been fascinated to see that she could keep her breath under the water for more than a few minutes. Not many air dwellers could. They swam around gentle fish, and played hide and seek around undersea boulders. Then noting how tired she must be feeling, he motioned for her to join him above water.

She swam upwards and he sped up to join her. He came above water just in front of her. She bounced in the water, floating effortlessly. He admired her stamina also. She shook the water out of her hair and palmed it out of her face, giving him a big grin filled with joyful playfulness.

"These waters are refreshing, but I would like to rest a little on the beach."

"Let's swim back there then."

He stayed close to her until their feet touched the sandy bottom of the seabed. Her hand went out to his and he clasped it in his own, happy to tread through the water with her at his side. They collapsed on the beach chuckling together. They then turned over on their backs to look up at the late afternoon sky. The sun wasn't too harsh this afternoon, it being mid-spring season and the breezes balmy.

"Your world is so beautiful. I've never seen such blue-green seas with such incredible life forms and I've seen many even on my world. I could easily like it here."

He rolled over on his side, propping his head up with one hand while he glanced down at her. She looked so beautiful. His heart and body ached with need for her.

"I could get use to the sight of you being there day after day." Her face scrunched with perturbed thoughts. "Don't be saddened. I just know you've made a sudden change in my...life. Let's leave it at that, shall we? You've enough on your mind hoping to learn there were survivors from your ship. Right now, close your eyes and relax."

His voice seemed to have a soothing effect on her, because she did as he asked. He'd been in heat phase for awhile, but he'd been good about keeping it in a simmer-mode, for now. But when she lay there looking so softly feminine and temptingly luscious, Taroc couldn't help but lean over and softly rub his lips against her partially open ones.

Her soft mutter of pleasure was enough to tempt him even further to explore her delicious mouth. He pressed his lips down upon hers, kissing her more thoroughly, nearly inhaling the deliciousness of her full lips. She tasted like sea wine, hearty and salty-sweet.

He'd never tasted anything like her lips before. He wanted more. With a sigh, though, he drew back. Her eyes flew open, at first in surprise, then in wonder, then in understanding.

He did not want to press her, or make matters awkward between them. Still, he couldn't deny he wanted her, needed her. But that was a move she had to make first. If it was entirely up to him, he'd take her right then and there.

Taroc didn't want to scare her away, no matter how much he wanted to make fierce love to her. She moved her head slightly to get a better look at him. For a moment he stayed breathlessly still as she studied his face again; then a slow smile crept up her lips and her left hand went up to his face.

She stroked his cheek softly at first before she moved her hand up behind his head. He only hoped, but became just a bit surprised when she nudged his head towards her. He didn't stiffen; instead, lowered his face to hers and kissed her soundly.

When she opened her moist lips to his, he nearly lost control. His manhood hardened with need as she rolled to her side and lay fully against him.

Darea said nothing, but she didn't have to, he perfectly understood her invitation. One he didn't' intend to ignore. Groaning, he pulled her beneath him and kissed her deeply. Her arms wound tightly around his waist and her luscious body arched against him.

He hadn't read her invitation wrong at all, she wanted him too...

* * * *

When he leaned over and claimed her lips again, Darea knew she was lost in his sea spell of seduction; for like the waves from the sea that washed over them, so too had she felt the liquid fire of his desires encompass her body.

His touch made her feel as alive as the ocean of wonders in which they previously swam. His hands splayed over her breast, her stomach and even lower in his seductively heated exploration of her whole body. She explored the strength of his lean, muscular frame, excited by the way he felt beneath her hands; and more so as he touched her with a fiery tenderness. But when she showed her own fervor of need, he didn't hold back.

She didn't want him to. She wanted their lovemaking to go on and on. When they joined, it was like a tidal wave of lustful wonder, never seeming to end; but when it did, the calming waves of the sea eased the turbulent passion that had overtaken them. He held her close afterwards and she felt the completion of bliss in his arms.

Much later, they went for a quick dip in the early evening coolness of the sea, and then regretfully returned to the cottage. Darea was sad he didn't stay longer, but as he said he had things to take care of below sea, she understood, and hoped she would see him again tomorrow sometime. Perhaps, even before Professor Havendor arrived. She could only hope.

She ate a light dinner with Minae and Persai then excused herself to go to the guest room they'd allowed her to use during her stay. Darea glanced at the emergency pack that lay on the full-sized comfortable bed and went immediately towards it. She didn't open it again when she'd first got back from her swim with Taroc, but left it on the bed here then had joined Persai and Minae later on for lunch after she'd taken a short nap.

She was tired and yet fully alive after her time with Taroc. His lovemaking had been as fantastic and heatedly wonderful. She'd never felt such rapture with any other male. It both excited and perturbed her body, mind, and heart; and wistfully, she wished they had met under different circumstances.

She sighed and pulled the communicator out of the backpack. It had been off, yet it seemed undamaged. She wondered if anyone had tried to contact her; perhaps not her personally, but someone, anyone from the ship who might have gotten into the particular pod in which she'd escaped. There was only one way to find out. Darea turned on the communicator.

It bleeped and crackled. A signal light blinked on and off the small screen. Two messages had been sent to this device; but she knew all the communicators had the same emergency frequency.

Her fingers trembled as she slowly pushed in the receiving button. A static voice bellowed out to her. She listened to both messages.

Darea recognized the voice and froze. Others had survived.

Chapter Six

She knew her heart had cracked like a volcanic fissure when she heard the voice on the communicator. Her commander had survived; and so had several other crewmembers.

Darea was overjoyed that they had, without a doubt. She'd been torn with stress over her new-found feelings for Taroc. When disaster struck ones life, did destiny always throw that person in turmoil? Did one's heart go through the gut-wrenching, turbulent seas that hers did now?

She got up early the next morning, not sleeping too well. Part of her was ecstatic to know that her comrades had survived; that others of her race were well and alive. Yet, she wondered how Taroc and her friends would take it if she left. Did she have any other choice though?

She sighed and dressed in the emergency jumpsuit she had in the backpack, but threw a sleeveless tunic in a similar color over it that Persai and Minae had bought for her. Then she slipped on the half boots with flat heels over her toe coverings and was prepared for what would come her way.

Darea couldn't eat much breakfast, but tried to. Her stomach was in a puddle of nerves mixed with bloody relief at knowing her shipmates were coming here. She had debated whether to tell Minae and Persai, but felt she owed them that much.

Last night she'd used the communicator to speak to one of her shipmates. Second Commander Ethun Cormus, an old friend, and long ago lover of hers. He'd told her that the Main Commander had died, as far as he knew, but several others in dual pods like his had landed near Fentwi; the city that Minae came from.

He'd used his emergency com-device to try to contact others that might have escaped to safety. Ten others had checked in with him within the last few days; then she'd called him last night.

He and a few others had been rescued by some fishermen near Fentwi and then brought to the Science Center Hospital. There they had been treated well, though cautiously taken care of. Professor Havendor, the director of Alien Studies had been contacted by the hospital and then Minae had also called him about her and inquired about extraterrestrial beings also, not long after. Over breakfast she'd told Minae and Persai what she knew transpired.

The three of them had put the information together and assumed that the professor was bringing Darea's commander and perhaps a few others with him. Darea hoped so. She needed to see them, to know they were ok. Especially, before she decided upon anything else.

She'd hoped Taroc would come, but he didn't. Perhaps he was troubled in his own way about her being reunited with her people and didn't want to get in the way of that event. She hoped that was the case and he would come at least to say goodbye to her.

Something told her he had come to care for her also. She bit her lip, trying not to think about being with him. She forced thoughts of him out of her mind as, not long after breakfast, and earlier than expected, a chime was heard at the front entrance to Persai and Minae's healing shop.

Darea held her breath as the couple went to see who it was. The shop was not open this morning due to the arrival of the expected company, though on normal days she knew it was and they would have been upfront or in the workshop.

She sat waiting in the main company room for them to return. Perhaps it was just a customer or patient needing some emergency attention. Her instincts told her that wasn't the case, and the fact was confirmed when she heard several sets of booted feet entering the room. She stood up and turned around.

Relief and joy washed over her when she saw a tall, dark blonde haired man with gray eyes smiling at her. His lean body was dressed not in their ship's uniform but a brown half robe-shirt and trousers, similar in style to Persai's green tunic outfit.

Two other people were behind him, but she didn't recognize them, and assumed they were from Fentwi. One was male, with a long beard and knowledgeable eyes, the other was a middle aged woman wearing a loose lavender robe one might wear when visiting a friend. Both had dark red hair, similar to Miane's coloring, though the female had lavender streaks running through hers.

"Darea! Heavens it is good to see you!" Ethun walked swiftly over to her and gave her a quick friendly hug. "I'm so glad you contacted me. There are a dozen now that I know of that survived, most landed near Fentwi."

He told her about how the pods landed in the sea surrounding the port city of Fentwi and how they were rescued, much as he'd told her on the communications device. All of them were given more advanced translation devices than the one in the necklace she wore. His was an earpiece, she noted. He rattled off several names then seemed to recall his manners when the auburn haired man with the beard cleared his throat.

"This is Professor Xan Havendor, who made the arrangements for me to come here with him. Professor, Lieutenant Darea Suttan, our main exobiologst and language expert from the ship we were on."

"It is a pleasure to meet another of your, shipmates, Commander. My former colleague here, Minae, has told me much about you, what she could that is. This island and marriage agrees with her."

"That it does, Xan," the other woman said. "Since Xan is not minding his manners, my name is Doctor Lina Trang. I believe we have a similar occupation Lieutenant Suttan. I'm a doctor of alien culture and biology. Hopefully we can exchange information one day when you are settled in Fentwi."

The woman reached over and touched Darea's left shoulder then moved back a step. The greeting custom was still a bit strange, but she accepted it.

However, Professor Xan Havendor stuck out his hand. "I like your greeting custom that Commander Ethun showed us. Welcome to our world."

She chuckled and heartily shook his hand. "I hope our races can exchange much. I'm sure meeting aliens was as unusual and scary for your people too."

He nodded. "But much has happened in the last few days, Lieutenant."

"Quite a bit, Darea," Ethun said and sat down when the host and hostess did, along with the others on several of the sofa-like seats in the room. "I've contacted our superiors on Urtha, they are astounded some of us are alive. Our ship's last emergency signal was picked up and they've been out looking for survivors. Professor Havendor and Doctor Trang have not only been most hospitable, but I've met with their leaders also. It seems our world and theirs are in contact agreements."

"You mean a rescue and greeting party is being sent here?" Darea was overjoyed at the news. "That's incredible in so short a time."

"I thought so too, but Space Centra has been in contact with them for nearly two days now off and on. They'll be sending representatives in a few days. They are as ecstatic about meeting these people and exchanging cultural and technology with them. We would have been returned had they not wanted to come and that fact is what opened the door to this unique meeting of worlds."

"I'm quite intrigued to hear it also." Minae, who had been studying the group with her keen eyes, Darea noted, spoke up. "This really is incredible news. We've hoped for this day in our lifetime, professor."

Persai smiled at them all nodding too. "I have no doubt Miane would like to be in on that meeting. It is going to be quite an event."

All heads turned to him, but the professor spoke up first. "You would not mind her coming to Fentwi for a short while? I was hoping she could be there to see this. You also are welcome."

Persai shook his head. "I am needed here, sir, but I would gladly let Minae go there."

Minae tightened her hand over her husband's. "It would not bother you then? Truly?"

"Just come back home soon." He looked down at his wife with such love; Darea was slightly envious but also happy for Miane.

Miane didn't care who was in the room and she fiercely hugged him. "Yes, I'd love to go. But only for a few days, my friends."

Dr. Trang clapped her hands. "It shall be a joy to work and visit with you again, dear Minae. I know your old colleagues will be glad and as you were good with people we hoped you would help us with exchanges too. Sit in on the preliminaries and such."

"I should like that."

Darea let out a soft sigh, which did not go unnoticed, especially by Ethun. He turned to her, taking his hand in hers. "I trust you are well and glad to come back with us. We can leave as soon as tomorrow, when the boat is going back to the mainland."

She nodded. "I'm fine. Persai and Minae have taken good care of me. It's just so much has happened, but yes, I'll be glad to see my shipmates. I've been so worried."

Ethun patted her hand like an affectionate brother would. "Good."

As if Minae had felt some tension in the room, she stood. "Darea, would you help me get some refreshments? I'm parched myself."

Darea was thankful for the interruption, but the three newcomers agreed they would be glad for a cool beverage. Persai affirmed stating he would keep them entertained while the two women went to get the refreshments.

Darea quietly followed Minae into the kitchen and felt relieved for a quick break. She didn't know what troubled her so much. She knew she was more than overjoyed to know some of her shipmates were alive and that she could see them again; but deep down it was something else that bothered her. She felt as if a fissure had cracked open.

Minae's hand touching her right shoulder brought her back to the current situation. She smiled at the woman, who folded her arms, giving her a glance that would brook no argument.

"Ok what's wrong? I've come to note your feelings over the last day or so. I'm a partial empath so I can feel something troubles you, though I am sure you are overjoyed at seeing your people again."

Darea leaned against a kitchen counter for a moment, as Minae did. "I am, Minae, I won't lie to you. I've worried about whether they were alive or not. Now that I know, I am sad to leave here."

"You mean the island or our world?"

Darea cocked her head to one side. "Both."

"You've come to care for him, haven't you?"

Darea knew she spoke of Taroc and didn't want to lie to her new friend. "Yes. I feel as if my heart is cracking right now. We're so different and he hasn't really said…"

"But you saw it in his eyes and felt it in his heart, didn't you?"

Darea nodded. "I don't know what to do, Minae. It's all so confusing. He didn't even come by today."

"I believe Taroc thought you needed time with your friends by yourself. Maybe he believed you needed to be with them, to figure out things before he could say anything."

"I want to believe that. I have missed my friends also."

"Perhaps being amongst your people for a few days will give you a chance to know what you truly want and feel. It's been a whirlwind for you. Take time out to figure out where you want to go and what you want to do with your life now. It doesn't matter that you are from different cultures or even different worlds. If you truly care for Taroc and he for you, as I believe, you'll find a way to work things out. Persai and I did and believe me, we had quite a few obstacles to overcome. One day I hope to get a chance to tell you my life story, share things with you as a friend."

"I'd like that too, Minae. Thank you. I knew if anyone could help me decide what to do, you could. I'm glad we've become friends. One day soon, indeed, we shall exchange more. I think we'd better take in those refreshments now."

Minae smiled and nodded her agreement. Indeed, Darea thought, Minae had told her what she needed to hear. She had to go back with Ethun, Minae and the others to Fentwi. She had to see the other survivors, talk with them, and decide whether she wanted to go back to her world or be part of an exchange, be part of something here.

Darea hoped she had a chance to see Taroc again and feel his arms around her before she left. She put those thoughts out of her head as she helped Minae carry trays of refreshments back to the company-room. But inside she quaked with turbulent emotions both good and troubled. She just had to find out what was most important to her. She just hoped she made the right choice...

Chapter Seven

Taroc floatingly paced the second story balcony of his home beneath the sea. He'd just finished a family meal but did not stay around for sea-charades, as they sometimes played after dinner. Mostly it was for the entertainment of his younger siblings that his parents and older brother sat down and participated in them.

So lost in his own thoughts, he didn't hear someone swish up behind him until they were almost next to him. He twirled around in the water, startling a curious starkle fish nearby. The little golden cretin swam quickly away at the other person's approach.

He smiled wistfully up at his brother, who floated a few inches taller than himself, though their feet were level on the balcony flooring.

"Want to tell me what's troubling you?"

He'd tried to hide his emotions, but it became harder and harder to do, especially since Darea left the island. "I'm not good at keeping things from you, am I, Jeth?"

Jeth shook his black locks, though they mostly swished hard in the water. "Nope. I saw you some days ago swimming in the sea with that unusual woman. She's one of the ones who fell from the sky, isn't she? I mean our communications equipment is as advanced as land dwellers. And though we haven't gone to space yet, we do learn what goes on around our world."

"And in our sea-cities around Epauch." He ran a hand through his green locks. "I think I've fallen in love with a land dweller, Jeth. A most unusual woman."

"And one who is from a totally alien culture also. Makes it harder for you." Jeth stated, studying him with those keen black eyes of his.

Taroc nodded. "Then you don't approve or…"

"Nor do I disapprove. Our parents and siblings want you happy, Taroc. If this woman is meant to be your sea-mate, then yes, you have our approval. You don't need it. Just be sure of your heart."

"I am. But she's still in Fentwi, amongst other survivors. Her space ship crashed and I pulled her from her escape pod." Taroc explained to his brother as much as he could about Darea and her people.

He'd learned a lot over the last few days from Persai what was going on and just before Minae and Darea left, he'd visited Persai with his concerns. His long-time friend had agreed with him that it was best Darea went to Fentwi to know her friends and shipmates were fine, and to be able to contact her world. Taroc gave him a message for Darea but told him not to deliver it until she was ready to leave on the ship going back to the mainland.

She needed her time, and in a way he did too. The few days away from her would do them both good; Persai had agreed too. He trusted his friend. Yet, Taroc knew he'd fallen for the alien woman. None could ever hold his heart as she did. His heart felt like the roaring turbulent waves that often stormed in during the fall season of this area. He sighed again, but kept his resolve. He had to believe she would return to him, soon.

His brother laid a hand on his shoulder, the man's words confirming his choice. "If she cares as deeply for you as you care for her, then she will come to you. And if the fates have decreed that you two are meant to be with each other, then you know there is a way for her to live with you here or on land."

Taroc jerked his head upwards in surprise. "You would help me get approval for the cellular change if she does."

"When the time is right and she has made her choice. I want you to be happy, Taroc. If this woman is the one for you, I will use whatever clout and favors I have to get the approval for you or her to have the surgery that would allow her to live in our sea-world. You can not tell her until we've met her of course."

He chuckled and the smile in his brother's voice made him relax. "I shall agree to that. I just hope our parents and people will come to love her as much as I do."

"You know, I've been thinking it is about time our own race ventured into other realms. What do you think?"

Laughing, Taroc nodded. "We do have the technology though we have not used it. Perhaps even, as I have long hoped, we can meet with the Space Center in Fentwi. Minae used to work there."

"Though I only met her and Persai a few times, I liked them. Persai is a lucky man. I think perhaps I am envious of you both."

"You will find your sea-mate one day, brother. When she falls into your arms perhaps."

"Perhaps," his brother agreed and laughed.

"Thanks, Jeth. I think I shall further excuse myself. I promised Persai I would meet with him tonight."

"Does Minae return tonight too?"

He sadly shook his head. "She comes back tomorrow. I will let you know what transpires then. Thank you."

"Very well. I'll see you tomorrow then. Good night, Taroc."

After his brother went back into their home, Taroc gave a thrust upwards with his legs, as if taking a giant leap, and soared upwards into the water, intending to visit with Persai. *Right now,* his mind told him, *any bit of positive news would put my turbulent heart at rest.*

* * * *

Darea felt as if she'd been in a whirlwind of events over the last few days. She missed the island, but when she got to Fentwi with the others, her homesickness resurfaced and so had her prior tragedy. She had missed all her shipmates and mourned, as the other survivors had, for all their losses. On a good note, other survivors from the ship's destruction had been found in various parts of Epauch.

Most had been rounded up and brought to Fentwi. The Fentwians had treated all very well with no hidden agenda. It was as she hoped; and when the ship arrived from her world of Urtha, there had been much more joyous feelings between all her crewmates. The Fentwi delegates and others from Urtha had made a momentous step forward in alien cultural exchanges. It was a historic event—one that had, changed her life completely around.

Though former lovers, but still good friends. Ethun had noted her moody behavior and she finally told him the reason why. One or two others, single and without family like herself, had opted to stay on Epauch; he told her she had the choice too.

Darea knew she'd see him again, he'd made friends quickly with a female from Fentwi, but also other people. His amenable nature was one reason Ethun always stayed friends with most. She learned a lot from him and more importantly, he'd told her that their government was ecstatic to finally meet with another scientifically advanced race, but a friendly one at that, who like them, wanted to exchange info, trade, and make lasting allies.

It was what people of her world had dreamt about for a long time. The way it had come about would be a sad spot always, but the crew of her ship would long be remembered. The Fentwi had kindly even had a remembrance ceremony for them. In her gut, she knew that Epauch had been a destiny for others too, as well as herself.

Once she'd talked to Ethun, a few of her surviving crewmates, and a representative friend of Ethun's from Urtha, and the events were over with, Darea made her choice. She said goodbye to her crewmates, and returned a day earlier than expected with Miane, back to the island, and back to where her heart lay. Minae said she was welcome to live with them until she further decided what to do. She knew her new friend had called Persai, her husband, because the man met them in town the afternoon of their arrival back to the island.

Darea had hoped that Taroc had been there to greet her, but Persai told her he'd be there later that evening and had kept it a surprise about her return. She was glad now that he had. She'd brought some new clothing back with her from Fentwi, where Minae had shown her around when they could catch time to do so. She felt anxious while she waited for Taroc to arrive. Dressed in a soft gown of blue and gold, she wanted to appeal to him. Hell, she just wanted to run in to his arms. But now, it was his turn to make that move, to show her he wanted her to stay here on Epauch and in his heart.

Darea waited in the main room, When Taroc walked into the room with Persai that evening he looked totally surprised; handsome, yes, desirable, definitely. Then he let out a guttural yell as he saw her and quickly made his way to her. She saw Persai and Minae exit the room as she and Taroc threw their arms around each other.

He started kissing her even before he spoke to her. Taroc twirled her around in his arms, nearly crushing her against himself. "By the stars I've missed you. Don't ever leave me again, Darea!"

"I could never leave you or Epauch or the island now, Taroc. My home is where your heart is. I love it here…and I love you," she said between hugs and deep kisses.

"Ah, my sweet alien, I would have gone to the stars had I needed to, just to bring you back to me. I wanted to give you time, to know your own heart." He stopped squeezing her, but kept her in his arms. "I've missed you terribly. Even my brother Jeth is looking forward to meeting you."

She glanced at him curiously. "You knew I'd be back?"

"My heart said yes, but it conflicted with my mind. We've known each other such a short time…"

She put a finger to his lips, stopping his words. "Love creeps up on one when one least expects it. Sometimes, it may take a few **years,** some times just days. I knew before I left here what lay in my heart."

"I do love you, Darea. Will you make your life here with me? Perhaps one day we could visit your world if you like."

"I know that Minae, perhaps even Persai, would like that, my heart," she chuckled and pressed close to his heated body. "But yes, I should like that. Do the Jnaith wish to do that now? Can they?"

He smiled down at her, one of his hands going behind her hips and pushing her up closer to his lower torso intimately. "Yes, they do and that I'll tell you about, soon, but not right now. Right now, I'd like to take you for a very long walk or swim in the lagoon. Or more, if you'd like."

She sparkled with desire in his arms. "I should like that very much, my love. All of it, and you."

He scooped her up in his arms, not giving her a chance to retract her statement. "You're positive you won't mind being here? I just have to make sure, Darea. Since I first laid eyes upon you, I couldn't think coherently, couldn't get over the turbulent emotions you've caused in my heart, and in my body."

She touched a finger to his forehead then his heart. "I too felt the same. But unless it's weather-wise, my heart or mind will no longer be in turbulence. However, my body is a different matter. Think you can handle that, my dear sea-mate?"

His grin widened revealing his white teeth. She loved that smile and him. "You bet. And you're just about to find out more what a sea male can do, sweet alien."

Taroc carried her out of the cottage and into a sea of bliss.

The End